Every gerbil has its day....

"Exactly how did you make your first million, Mr. Bluett?" the reporter asks.

"I was in the breeding business."

"Horses?"

"No, gerbils."

"Oh, are you the one who made gerbils so popular?"

Jeremy smiles. *"My little business just grew and grew until gerbils were the most popular pets in the country. Why, you hardly ever see a dog anymore."*

"A dog?" The young reporter laughs. *"Do you mean people used to keep dogs as pets?"*

"Some people did," Jeremy says. *"Now everyone has a gerbil."*

GERMY
BLEW IT—AGAIN!

Rebecca C. Jones

BULLSEYE BOOKS • ALFRED A. KNOPF

New York

For David Crawford Jones,
who unknowingly introduced me
to Germy

———————

"*C*an I help set the table?" Jeremy asked.

Mrs. Bluett looked at Jeremy suspiciously. "Why?"

"I finished my homework early, and I just want to help."

His mother still looked wary. "I guess so."

Jeremy got out four yellow place mats and arranged them around the table. Then he set out the plates and glasses. He folded the napkins carefully and placed the silverware on them.

"Is there anything else I can do?" he asked.

His mother tilted her head and eyed him closely. "Is there something wrong?" she asked.

"No, nothing's wrong." Jeremy smiled.

"Did Mrs. Scheeler send a note home with you again?"

Jeremy shook his head.

"You forgot to do your homework?" she guessed. "You were chewing gum in class again? You signed me up to bake three dozen cupcakes for a class party?"

Jeremy kept shaking his head.

"I give up," she said. "What is it?"

"Nothing's wrong," he said again. "I just think I'm old enough to help more around the house."

"Well, I can't argue with that."

Jeremy went out to the family room and found Robin doing her math. He remembered how hard math was when he was in third grade.

"Do you need any help?" he asked.

"No," she said. "This is simple."

At dinner Jeremy told his father that the advertisements in *The Advocate-Journal* looked particularly nice tonight.

"Really?" said Mr. Bluett, who worked in the advertising department at the newspaper. "I'll have to look at them again."

"I can see a lot of creativity in them," Jeremy said. "They're even more creative than the news stories." He knew his father would rather be a reporter, but the advertising job paid more.

"The news isn't supposed to be creative," Mr. Bluett said. "It's supposed to be true."

"And this stir-fry," Jeremy said, nodding at the mixture on his fork. "It's the best I've ever tasted."

"Why, thank you, Jeremy," Mrs. Bluett said.

Robin looked down at her plate. "It tastes the same as always to me," she said.

"Maybe so," Jeremy said. "It's just that sometimes I forget what a terrific cook Mom is."

Both of his parents stopped eating.

"All right, Jeremy," Mr. Bluett said. "Suppose you tell us what's going on."

"I don't know what you're talking about," Jeremy said.

"Excuse me for being suspicious," his father said. "But I haven't heard you compliment the cooking around here since the days when you were trying to get out of violin lessons."

Mrs. Bluett looked wistful, the way she always did when somebody mentioned Jeremy's old violin lessons.

"I'm just trying to show a little maturity," Jeremy said.

"He needs money," Robin said.

"Oh, that." Mrs. Bluett started eating again.

They all knew--everybody at Dolley Madison Elementary School knew--that Jeremy owed the school $10.55. He had been in charge of a bubble gum blowing contest that was supposed to raise money for the school, but he used some of the entry fees to buy bags of Big Bubba bubble gum for himself.

"We've already told you, Jeremy, that you'll have to pay the school out of your own money," Mr. Bluett said.

"He doesn't have any money," said Robin, who liked to keep track of things.

"Not any?" Mrs. Bluett looked at Jeremy. "What about your allowance? And the money Grandma gave you at Christmas?"

"I spent it," Jeremy said.

"All of it?" she asked.

Jeremy nodded.

His mother sighed, and his father shook his head. "I guess you'll just have to start saving your allowance," he said.

Jeremy moaned. His allowance was so puny—just a dollar a week—that he would be an old man before he saved $10.55.

"Of course, there's one way you could get the money faster," Mr. Bluett said.

"You could raise my allowance?"

"Guess again."

Jeremy pretended not to know what his father meant.

"You could *earn* the money," Mr. Bluett said finally. "When I was your age, I had a paper route."

Jeremy knew. He'd heard his father's stories about getting up at 5 A.M., riding his bike through blizzards, and fending off mad dogs.

"I don't think Mrs. Lounsberry would give up her route for Jeremy," Mrs. Bluett said.

Good old Mrs. Lounsberry.

"But there must be other jobs in the neighborhood," his father said. "The idea is to find a need and fill it. That's how the free enterprise system works."

"I'll tell you what *we* need," Mrs. Bluett said. "We need somebody to shovel our sidewalk. I nearly broke my neck when I came home from work this afternoon."

"That's it," Mr. Bluett said. "You could shovel sidewalks."

"Beginning with ours," Mrs. Bluett said.

Jeremy had shoveled sidewalks before.

"That's too boring," he said. "And it takes too much time."

"Slow and steady wins the race," Mr. Bluett said.

"I'm not the slow and steady type," Jeremy said.

His mother sighed again. "We know."

⟋⟍

After dinner Jeremy went out to the family room and found Robin studying the Sears Wish Book.

4

"Christmas is over," he reminded her.

"I know," she said. "I'm going to *buy* that." She pointed to a picture of a fish tank in the catalog. "And then maybe I'll buy some angelfish at the pet store. And maybe some neon tetra, too. Of course, I can't buy everything at once. I only have twenty-three dollars and sixty-four cents."

Jeremy sighed. If he had $23.64, he wouldn't waste it on a dumb old fish tank. He'd use it to buy baseball cards and posters of rock singers and bags of Big Bubba bubble gum.

And he'd pay the school, too.

Robin smiled as she closed the catalog. "Maybe I won't buy anything at all. Maybe I'll just keep saving until I have a hundred dollars. Or a thousand." She tapped her fingers on the catalog. "I wonder what I could buy with a thousand dollars."

She probably wouldn't buy anything, Jeremy thought. She'd probably just keep saving, until she had a million dollars. Or maybe a billion.

Robin looked at him. "Are you going to start a sidewalk shoveling business?" she asked.

"No," Jeremy said. "I've got other plans."

Jeremy didn't know what his other plans were yet. But they had to be better than shoveling sidewalks.

A newspaper reporter comes into Jeremy's office and sits down. "Tell me, Mr. Bluett," he says, "have you always been the world's richest man?"

Jeremy laughs. "Oh, no," he says. "I started out deeply in debt. I even owed the school money. Things were so bad that my parents suggested I shovel snow from sidewalks in the neighborhood."

5

"Did you?"

Jeremy laughs again and shakes his head. "I had much bigger plans."

The reporter looks around the lavishly furnished office. "I guess you did. Nobody could build this kind of empire by shoveling sidewalks."

2

*M*rs. Bluett slipped on the icy top step in the morning.

"Jeremy," she said as she caught herself on the railing, "I want you to take care of this as soon as you get home this afternoon. It'll be good practice for your sidewalk shoveling business."

"But I'm not—"

"Can I do it, Mom?" Robin asked.

"I don't care who does it," Mrs. Bluett said. "Just as long as it gets done."

Jeremy smiled. Robin probably thought Mom and Dad would pay her extra for scraping the ice off the front steps. Evidently she hadn't heard the lecture about pitching in and helping the family out of the goodness of her heart.

Mrs. Bluett drove them to school. When Jeremy got out of the car, he saw Squirrel Hutchison standing with Kevin Johansen by the chain link fence that separated Dolley Madison Elementary School from the Titus-Sadler Funeral Home.

"Germy!" Squirrel called. "Come here!"

Only teachers and new kids called Jeremy Bluett by his real name. Everyone else at school called him Germy Blew It.

"Look what Kevin's got," Squirrel said. "A whole carton of Twinkies. And they're not even smushed."

Kevin's father drove a Hostess delivery truck, so Kevin usually brought damaged desserts to school in his lunch.

"I'm going to sell them at lunchtime," Kevin said. "For just forty-five cents a package. That's less than you'd pay in a store."

"Geez Louise," Squirrel said. "I wish I'd brought some money with me today."

"Don't worry about it," Kevin said, jingling some coins in his pocket. "You can pay me tomorrow."

Jeremy stuck his hands into his own empty pockets. "Can I pay tomorrow, too?" he asked.

Kevin stopped jingling. "No way."

"Why not? You're letting Squirrel do it."

"Squirrel doesn't owe the school fifteen or twenty dollars," Kevin said.

"Neither do I," Jeremy said. Then he added softly, "I just owe ten dollars and fifty-five cents."

Kevin laughed.

"That's okay, Germy," Squirrel said. "I'll give you one of my Twinkies."

But Jeremy didn't want Squirrel's charity. He wanted to

buy his own Twinkies. And he wanted to jingle coins in his pocket, too.

❧

"Exactly how poor were you, Mr. Bluett?" the reporter asks.

"I couldn't even afford a package of Twinkies that a kid was selling for forty-five cents. He let other kids buy on credit, but not me."

The reporter laughs. "That's hard to believe, sir. Do you know what ever happened to that kid who wouldn't let you have a Twinkie?"

"Yes, I employ him at one of my mansions. He's in charge of cleaning toilet bowls. I have thirty-seven toilets at that mansion, and I insist that every one of them be cleaned twice a day."

"Wow," the reporters says, "that's a lot of toilet bowl cleaning!"

❧

"What's in the box?" Mrs. Scheeler asked when the boys walked into her fifth grade classroom.

"Twinkies," Kevin said.

"Twinkies?"

"They're forty-five cents a package." Kevin smiled like a salesman. "That's less than you'd pay in a store."

"You're going to sell these at school?" Mrs. Scheeler asked.

Still smiling, Kevin nodded. "Do you want to buy some?"

"That's not what I had in mind," she said. "Please put the box next to my desk. You can have it back at three o'clock."

Kevin stopped smiling. "Why?" he asked. "What's wrong?"

"You're not allowed to sell things on school property," Mrs. Scheeler said. "Now put it next to my desk."

Jeremy tried to look sympathetic as Kevin carried the carton to Mrs. Scheeler's desk. But inside Jeremy was grinning.

"That's not fair," Kevin muttered as he came back to his seat. "My dad gave them to me, and I should be able to do anything I want with them."

"Don't worry about it," Squirrel said. "You can sell them after school in front of the funeral home."

That's right, Jeremy thought. Kevin would be able to sell them all after school. And he'd make a killing.

Jeremy stopped grinning on the inside.

He worried about his finances all day. On the math worksheet, a boy named Jim owed Harold $4.05. He owed Peter $3.36, and he owed Matthew $3.12. When Jeremy added up the figures, he found that Jim owed his friends $10.53—just two cents less than Jeremy owed the school.

Poor Jim. There was no way he was going to be able to pay back Harold, Peter, and Matthew. And there was no way Jeremy was going to be able to pay back the school—not unless Mr. Bluett started bringing home cartons of Twinkies for Jeremy to sell.

On the way to the cafeteria at noon, Jeremy saw Ms. Morrison, the school principal.

"Hello, Jeremy," she said. "How are you today?"

"Don't worry," he said. "I'll get the money."

She looked puzzled for a moment, then smiled. "Oh, that." She put an arm around Jeremy's shoulder, so she was hugging him, *hugging* him, right in the middle of the school corridor.

Jeremy should have known this would happen. Ms. Morrison was always hugging first and second graders. Sometimes she got carried away and did it with older kids, too. Especially if she thought they were having Problems. She probably thought Jeremy was having a Problem because he owed the school money.

"I have complete confidence in you, Jeremy," Ms. Morrison was saying, with her hands clamped around his shoulders. "You're the most industrious boy I know."

"Uh, thanks," Jeremy said, trying to squirm away. Out of the corner of his eye, he saw Kevin, watching.

But Ms. Morrison held on tight. "You're developing into a fine young man, Jeremy."

If she'd only stop hugging him.

"I'm late for lunch," Jeremy hinted.

Finally she let go. "Well, then, hurry along."

"Yeah, Germy," Kevin said in a falsetto voice from behind him, "hurry along! Unless you want to go kissy-face with the principal some more."

Jeremy walked quickly, but Kevin caught up with him. "I know how you could make money, Germy," he said. "You could open a kissing booth. A dollar a kiss. I bet Ms. Morrison would be your biggest customer. Then you could afford all the Twinkies you want."

⌒∽

Squirrel had saved a seat for Jeremy in the cafeteria.

"I've got to think of a way to make money," Jeremy said as he sat down. "Fast."

"Why don't you ask your parents?"

"I already did."

"And they won't give it to you?" Squirrel shook his head. "Geez Louise."

They both knew Squirrel's parents would give him the money if he needed it. His parents were nice that way.

"I wish I could think of something to sell," Jeremy said.

"You could sell your posters," Squirrel suggested. "I'd buy Bruce Springsteen if you could get him off your wall without ripping him too much."

"No," Jeremy said. "Not my posters."

"How about your baseball cards?" Squirrel asked. "Remember that guy who offered you fifty bucks for your Willie Mays rookie card?"

Jeremy had found a 1952 Willie Mays card in a box of baseball cards he bought at a garage sale. When the man at Cherry's Collectibles saw the card, he offered Jeremy fifty dollars for it. He said the card would be worth a lot more if it were in mint condition, without the brown spots that looked like somebody had spilled Coke on it.

"That was a long time ago," Jeremy said.

"Right," Squirrel said. "The card's probably worth even more now."

Jeremy nodded. Even with the Coke stains, Willie Mays's card was the best one in his collection. Heck, nobody at Dolley Madison Elementary School had a better baseball card. Not even Kevin Johansen.

"I can't sell Willie," Jeremy said. "No way."

"Well, what are you willing to sell?"

Jeremy thought about it. "My violin," he said.

"Your violin?" Squirrel shook his head. "Forget it. Nobody'll want to buy that thing."

"Maybe a kid wouldn't," Jeremy said, "but some mother might." He remembered how excited his own mother had been when he first started taking Suzuki lessons.

"Just don't tell *my* mother it's for sale," Squirrel said.

"Don't worry," Jeremy said. "It's a small violin. For little kids."

"Still," Squirrel said. "I don't want her getting any ideas."

∽

After lunch Mrs. Scheeler told everyone to open their social studies books to page 137. They were beginning a chapter on The Industrialists. Jeremy would have read it the night before if he had remembered to take his book home.

"Jeremy," Mrs. Scheeler said, "who is Andrew Carnegie?"

Carnegie, Carnegie. Jeremy had heard that name before. Other kids waved their hands in the air.

Mrs. Scheeler sighed. "All right, Mary Kate. Tell us about Andrew Carnegie."

Mary Kate Williams smiled at Jeremy. "Andrew Carnegie came to this country as a poor immigrant boy," she said, "but he made a huge fortune as a steel manufacturer. Then he gave millions of dollars to libraries, schools, and other charities."

"Thank you, Mary Kate," Mrs. Scheeler said. "You would have known that, too, Jeremy, if you'd read your assignment."

∽

"I think what I admire most about you, Mr. Bluett," the reporter says, "is the way you've spent your fortune. You've contributed to so many schools, libraries, hospitals, and other worthwhile projects."

Jeremy smiles modestly. "I haven't contributed much to schools," he says. "I've never considered them very worthwhile."

13

3

A crowd gathered around Kevin and his box of Twinkies in front of the funeral home after school. One kid took a bite out of his Twinkie and complained that it was stale.

Jeremy grinned when he heard that, but he didn't stop. He had to hurry to Mrs. Carlson's house.

He and Robin always went to Mrs. Carlson's after school. Normally Jeremy hated going there because Mrs. Carlson wouldn't let him watch television, use the telephone, or play with Squirrel.

But today he was glad to be going there. Five other kids stayed at Mrs. Carlson's house, and they were all younger than Jeremy. Today they all looked like little violinists.

"Donnie," Jeremy said to a four-year-old marching two

Keen Marine figures across the kitchen table, "have you ever thought about becoming a concert violinist?"

"Bam-bam-bam," Donnie Klondaris said. "You're dead!" One of the Keen Marines fell off the table.

"You could make lots of money," Jeremy said, "and buy lots of Keen Marines."

Donnie looked at him.

"But you have to start now," Jeremy said. "You have to start taking violin lessons."

"Lin lessons?" Donnie asked.

"*Vio*-lin lessons," Jeremy said. "You have to tell your mom you want to play the *vio*-lin."

"*Vio*-lin," Donnie repeated. "*Keen* Marine."

"That's right," Jeremy said. "If you play the violin, you'll get a Keen Marine. So you tell your mom to call this number." Jeremy scribbled his phone number on the back of an old math test. "And I'll sell her a *violin*. Real cheap."

Donnie took the math test and nodded. "Real cheap."

Betty Lou Walker seemed interested in the violin, too, especially after Jeremy hinted that she might star in her own MTV video.

And Sabrina Murphy liked the idea of wearing a bright pink evening gown—just like a Barbie doll's—to the violin concerts.

"Don't forget to tell your moms that they can buy my old violin real cheap," Jeremy said, giving them both old test papers with his phone number scribbled on the backs.

Betty Lou and Sabrina nodded and took the papers.

Mrs. Bluett arrived to pick up Jeremy and Robin before he had a chance to talk to the other kids. It didn't matter, though. After all, he had only one violin.

Jeremy wondered how much he should charge for it.

His mother had told him often enough that the violin had cost $275. But he had used it for two years, so it probably wasn't worth that much now.

Maybe he should charge two hundred dollars.

Jeremy thought of all the things he could buy with two hundred dollars. He could buy Twinkies anytime he wanted. He could buy enough rock posters to paper all four walls of his bedroom. He could buy this year's baseball cards all at once, instead of getting them in dribs and drabs. Heck, he could buy a ticket to some—maybe all—of the World Series games.

And he'd pay the school, too.

∾

"Could you tell me the secret to your success, Mr. Bluett?" *the reporter asks.*

Jeremy smiles modestly. "Gee, I don't know. I've just always tried to do what is right."

"You certainly have," the reporter says. "Everyone knows that Jeremy Bluett always pays his debts."

Jeremy smiles again, even more modestly.

∾

Jeremy did his homework by the telephone. He looked out the window and saw Robin shoveling the front steps. Her face was red from the cold.

Jeremy felt a little guilty. Here he was, sitting nice and warm by the telephone, just waiting for it to ring so he could collect two hundred dollars. And there was Robin, chipping away at the ice, hoping Mom and Dad would pay her.

Somebody should tell her the truth.

He went to the front door and opened it a crack.

"Robin," he said kindly, "I think I should tell you. Mom and Dad aren't going to pay you for this."

"I know," Robin said, without looking up. "But I need the practice."

What a weird kid, Jeremy thought, as he shut the door and went back to his post by the telephone.

Mrs. Klondaris called at 5:15.

"Jeremy?" she said. "Donnie tells me you're selling your old Keen Marines."

"No," Jeremy said. "I'm selling a violin."

"A violin? But Donnie said you had lots of old Keen Marines that you wanted to get rid of. He said you were selling them cheap."

"No," Jeremy said again. "I'm selling a violin."

"Do you have *any* Keen Marines?"

"No," Jeremy said for the third time. *"I'm selling a violin."*

Mrs. Klondaris sighed. "Donnie's not going to be happy about this." Then she hung up.

Sabrina Murphy's mother called after dinner, wanting to buy Barbie clothes. She wasn't interested in a violin, either.

Jeremy decided little kids didn't make good messengers. He'd better try to sell his violin directly to adults. Maybe he could take it door-to-door to the mothers in his neighborhood. He could even take the violin out of its case and play "Go Tell Aunt Rhody" as a demonstration.

If he wanted "Go Tell Aunt Rhody" to sound good, he'd better practice it. He went upstairs and found the violin case on the top shelf in the back of his closet, under the pumpkin costume he'd worn in the second grade class play. He pulled over the chair from his desk so he could reach it.

He put the case on his bed and opened it. The violin looked smaller than he remembered.

He tucked it under his chin and drew the bow across the strings. The violin screeched. It didn't sound at all like "Go Tell Aunt Rhody."

"What was that?" Mrs. Bluett appeared at his door. "Oh, my goodness," she breathed when she saw the violin.

Jeremy quickly put the violin back in its case. He didn't like the look on his mother's face.

"Don't let me stop you," she said. "I *knew* you'd come back to the violin someday. That's why I never got rid of it. But, of course, now you need a larger one." She smiled and cocked her head as if she could hear Jeremy in an orchestra.

Jeremy snapped the violin case shut and put it back on the top shelf of his closet. He buried it under the pumpkin costume again. He had forgotten what a dangerous instrument this violin was.

Somebody would just have to buy the violin on faith, without ever hearing "Go Tell Aunt Rhody."

4

*M*rs. Bluett gave Jeremy and Robin their allowances on Friday afternoon.

"Don't spend this right away," Mrs. Bluett said as she handed Jeremy his dollar. "Remember to save some of it for your school debt."

"Don't worry," Jeremy said. Once he sold his violin, he knew he'd be rolling in money.

Mrs. Bluett looked at her watch. "I wonder if we have time to go to the store before dinner."

"Findley's?" Jeremy asked hopefully.

His mother nodded.

Jeremy loved going to Findley's Fine Foods. He liked the wide aisles, the rows of colorful packages, and the piped-in music. Sometimes Mr. Findley himself interrupted the music to announce "another Fine Findley Bargain under the flashing green light on Aisle 13."

Jeremy always hurried over to the flashing light, but the Fine Findley Bargain was usually for something like toilet paper or tomato sauce. Once, though, the Fine Findley Bargain was a Keen Marine ruler, which Jeremy bought for the low, low price of twenty-nine cents before he remembered that Keen Marines were dumb. He kept the ruler in his desk at home, because he didn't want anyone at school to think that he still liked Keen Marines.

The best part of Findley's was the row of glass-bulbed machines near the front door. For a quarter or fifty cents, you could buy anything from a jawbreaker to a rabbit's-foot key chain.

Jeremy's favorite machine sold miniature plastic football helmets for a quarter. Jeremy hoped to collect the helmets from all twenty-eight NFL teams, but this was tricky because you couldn't pick the helmet you wanted. You just had to take what the machine gave you. The machine at Findley's gave out a lot of Miami Dolphins helmets. Jeremy had six of them, but he'd never gotten a single Cincinnati Bengals helmet.

Everybody had trouble getting Bengals helmets. The only person who had one was Kevin Johansen, and he got his because his father knew the man who serviced the machines. Jeremy figured that's what happened to all the Bengals helmets: Somebody pulled them out before filling the machines.

But two weeks ago Jeremy had spotted a Bengals helmet that had evidently slipped into the machine by mistake. It was at the top of the glass bulb then, and by last week it had traveled halfway down to the opening. Maybe today the Bengals helmet would be down at the bottom, ready to come out.

Jeremy knew from experience that the machine always covered the next three or four helmets it would dispense. So it was a good sign today when he couldn't see the Bengals helmet.

While Mrs. Bluett squeezed grapefruit in the produce section, Jeremy stood in the express checkout lane to get change for his dollar bill.

Robin wandered over. "What are you doing?" she asked.

"Nothing," Jeremy said.

Robin looked around and spotted the machines. "Which one are you going for?" she asked.

"Football helmets," he said. "I need the Bengals."

The clerk gave him four quarters, and they walked over to the football helmet machine.

"I don't see the Bengals," Robin said.

"It's down at the bottom, ready to come out."

"How do you know that?"

"I know this machine," Jeremy said. "I've studied it."

He put a quarter in the machine. Out came the New York Giants.

"Don't you already have a Giants helmet?" Robin asked.

Jeremy didn't say anything. He just dropped another quarter into the machine. This time he got the Washington Redskins.

"You already have the Redskins, too," Robin chirped.

Another quarter, and the Los Angeles Rams fell into his hand.

Jeremy looked at the last quarter in his hand.

"Don't do it, Jeremy," Robin said. "I bet they don't even *make* Bengals helmets."

Jeremy looked at the machine. He knew the Bengals helmet was in there, just waiting for him.

Unless some other kid had already gotten it.

"Do you have any advice for young businessmen, Mr. Bluett?" the reporter asks.

"Show courage," Jeremy says. "If you don't believe in yourself, no one else will."

He shoved his last quarter into the slot. Out dropped a Miami Dolphins helmet.

"Oh," Robin said softly. "You have *lots* of those."

"What's in your pocket, Jeremy?" Mrs. Bluett asked as they carried grocery bags to the car.

"Old football helmets," Jeremy said. The helmets might as well be old, he thought.

Still, he glanced at Robin, whose face was hidden by a bag bulging with paper towels.

"Football helmets?" Mrs. Bluett looked puzzled.

"You know, those little plastic helmets I used to collect." He kept his eyes on the paper towels.

"Oh, those things," Mrs. Bluett said, shifting her bags as she fumbled for her car keys. "I always thought they were such a waste of money."

The paper towels didn't say a thing, and Jeremy felt grateful.

5

"Snow!" Robin squealed as she ran into Jeremy's room the next morning. "There's fresh snow on the ground!"

Jeremy sat up quickly and reached for the radio. Maybe the school superintendent would call off school. Then he remembered it was Saturday.

"So what?" he said as he slid back under the covers. "We don't have school today anyway."

But Robin was still excited. "Fresh snow!" she cried as she ran out of his room.

By the time Jeremy shuffled downstairs for breakfast, Robin was gone.

"I have to admire the kid's spunk," his father was saying.

Jeremy stopped shuffling and put a little extra spunk into his walk.

"Yes, she's certainly industrious," his mother said.

She? Jeremy went back to shuffling.

"Good morning, sleepyhead," Mrs. Bluett said.

"Who's spunky?" Jeremy asked.

"Robin," his father said. "She's out there shoveling the sidewalk."

"And she didn't even ask if we'd pay her," Mrs. Bluett marveled.

"Why should she?" Jeremy asked. "You never paid me for doing it."

"Or me, either." Mr. Bluett sighed. "When I think of all the work I've done around this place . . ."

"Which reminds me." Mrs. Bluett smiled at her husband. "The water heater is making a funny noise again."

"Me and my big mouth."

ᘓ

After breakfast Jeremy went upstairs to get his violin. He waited until his parents were looking at the water heater before he brought the violin downstairs. Then he quickly put on his jacket and went outside.

Robin was just finishing the sidewalk.

"Where are you going with your violin?" she asked.

"I've got some business to take care of," he said.

Robin looked interested. "What kind of business?"

"Never mind," Jeremy said as he surveyed the houses on the street. A lot of the houses had old people in them, and he knew they wouldn't be interested in such a small violin.

His eyes stopped on the Cavanaughs' house. They had four kids, all younger than Robin; maybe Mrs. Cavanaugh would like one of them to play the violin.

Even before he reached the Cavanaughs' driveway, he could hear the noise. A television set was blasting out "Adventures of Space Monkey," and it sounded like at least seventeen kids were arguing over the possession of a police whistle found in a box of Chewy Crunch Breakfast Cereal.

Timmy Cavanaugh answered the door. Jeremy knew, from his experience with Donnie Klondaris and Sabrina Murphy, that he'd better talk directly to Mrs. Cavanaugh.

"I want to talk to your mother!" Jeremy shouted over the argument about the police whistle.

"It's Saturday!" Timmy yelled back.

"So?"

"My mother went to get some peace and quiet at the grocery store," Timmy explained. "But my dad's here."

"May I speak with him?"

Timmy left the door open while he went in search of his father. Jeremy knew what his own parents would say about leaving the door open on such a cold day. He wondered whether he should shut it—and whether he should step inside to do so. He decided to stay outside, with the door open.

"Timmy!" Mr. Cavanaugh yelled when he arrived. "You left the door open!" He turned to Jeremy. "What can I do for you?"

"I wondered if you'd like—"

The police whistle blew.

"What?" Mr. Cavanaugh shouted.

"I wondered if you'd like to buy a violin!" Jeremy shouted back.

"A violin!" Mr. Cavanaugh looked over his shoulder and groaned. "That's all I need."

Jeremy met Robin, dragging her snow shovel, on the Cavanaughs' driveway.

"What are you doing here?" he asked.

"I've got some business to take care of," she said, passing him.

"What kind of business?"

"Never mind," she called back over her shoulder. "You've got your business, and I've got mine."

Jeremy went across the street to the Gerards'. They had just one little girl, so their house was a lot quieter.

"Hello, Mrs. Gerard," Jeremy said. "Would you like to buy a violin for Melissa?"

"I'm sorry, Jeremy," Mrs. Gerard said. "Melissa already plays the piano and the flute. She just doesn't have time for another instrument." She looked at the violin case. "I remember your mother showing me that violin. It's a beautiful instrument. Are you sure you want to sell it?"

Jeremy nodded. "I need the money."

"Surely there must be another way. Surely your parents—"

"No," Jeremy said. "They can't help me."

"I'm sorry to hear that."

When Jeremy turned to go, he saw that Robin was at the Cavanaughs', shoveling snow from their front sidewalk.

"What are you doing?" Jeremy called to her.

"What does it look like?" she called back.

He skipped Donnie Klondaris's and Sabrina Murphy's houses because he knew they didn't want a violin; they just wanted Keen Marines and Barbie dolls.

His feet were cold, and he wished he'd worn his boots. He kept one hand in his pocket, but the other one, holding the violin case, was beginning to grow numb from the cold.

Still, he didn't stop. He went around the corner and tried Betty Lou Walker's house.

"Yes," Mrs. Walker said, "Betty Lou told me you were selling a violin."

Good old Betty Lou. It was nice to know there was at least one four-year-old in the world who could get a message straight.

Mrs. Walker smiled. "You know, I took violin lessons when I was a child."

Jeremy forgot the cold. He smiled back at her.

"And I've always hated the instrument. I don't think I could stand hearing that thing screech again."

Jeremy skipped Squirrel's house and continued around the block, looking for a house with a music-loving mother in it. He saw a car with a BABY ON BOARD sign on the rear window, so he stopped at that house and rang the doorbell. But the baby was just four months old and not ready for music lessons yet.

"Check with us in three or four years," the mother said.

"Make that eight or ten," the father called from behind her.

Jeremy saw a FOR SALE sign in front of one house. Maybe a music-loving mother would move in and want a violin for her children.

But that might take a long time, and Jeremy needed money now.

6

*R*obin shoveled snow all morning and most of the afternoon. She made twenty dollars.

"Twenty dollars!" Jeremy breathed.

Maybe he should have shoveled snow.

"That means I have forty-three dollars and sixty-four cents," Robin said. "Think of what I can buy."

But Jeremy didn't want to think of that. He wanted to think of the two hundred dollars he'd get once he sold his violin.

But he hadn't sold his violin yet.

Maybe he should look for a buyer outside his neighborhood. Maybe he should advertise in *The Advocate-Journal.*

He went down to the family room, where his father was reading *The Cleveland Plain Dealer.* Mr. Bluett always brought out-of-town newspapers home on the weekend so he could see what their advertising departments were doing.

Jeremy found a copy of *The Advocate-Journal* and opened it to a full-page picture of a woman with long hair and a shopping cart. COME WITH ME! the words next to her said. I SHOP AT FINDLEY'S FINE FOODS!

Jeremy could see it now: a full-page picture of himself playing his violin. PLAY WITH ME! the words would say. I APPEAR IN CONCERTS ALL OVER THE COUNTRY!

Of course, Jeremy didn't appear in concerts all over the country. But he bet that woman with the long hair didn't shop at Findley's, either. That was just advertising.

"Dad," Jeremy said.

Mr. Bluett rustled his newspaper.

"Dad," Jeremy said again.

"Did you say something?" Mr. Bluett asked.

"How much would an ad like this cost?" Jeremy pointed to the woman with the long hair and the shopping cart.

"Oh, about fifteen hundred bucks."

"Wow." Mr. Findley must be rich.

Jeremy figured he couldn't afford one of the smaller ads that took up a half page or so, either. Then he spotted a tiny ad at the bottom of page thirty-three. FINAL CLOSE-OUT, it said, GOLDER'S FASHION JEWELRY, 1116 N. BROAD ST.

Maybe he could afford something like that. LAST VIO-LIN, it would say, along with his address and telephone number.

"How much would this cost?" Jeremy asked, pointing to the ad.

"Hmmmm?" Mr. Bluett rustled his newspaper again.

"How much would this cost?" Jeremy asked again.

Mr. Bluett looked at the ad. "About twenty-five dollars."

"Oh."

Jeremy's father put down his newspaper. "Is something wrong?"

"Well, I have this friend who wants to sell something. He was thinking about putting an ad in the newspaper, but it's just too expensive."

"Why doesn't he take out a classified ad?"

"A classified ad?"

Mr. Bluett flipped through the newspaper to its back pages, which were filled with tiny print. "The big ads are mainly for businesses and political candidates. Regular people advertise in the classifieds."

"But these are so small," Jeremy said. "Nobody can read them."

"Nobody can read *all* of them," Mr. Bluett corrected him. "But lots of people read parts of them. Let's say you want to buy a pet." He turned a couple of pages. "Here we are. *Pets*. You just read through these until you find the pet you want."

"Pet?" Robin appeared, just like she always did whenever someone mentioned something furry. "Did you say we're getting a pet?"

"No, Robin," Mr. Bluett said. "That's just an example. I was showing Jeremy how to read the classified ads."

"Look," Jeremy said, reading. "Some of these pets are free."

"Free?" Robin came over to look.

Jeremy pointed to the ad.

FREE BEAGLE to loving home. 1 yr old, great with kids. Owner allergic. 555-6842 after 5 p.m.

"A free beagle!" Robin cried. "I've always wanted a free beagle!"

Her father sighed. "Now look what you've started," he said to Jeremy.

"But this is a real bargain," Jeremy said. "Look, here's another beagle that costs two hundred and fifty dollars."

"Just think," Robin said. "We could save two hundred and fifty dollars by getting the free one."

"Sally!" Mr. Bluett called to his wife. "It's time to do our old song and dance!"

"The one about the dog?" Mrs. Bluett called from the kitchen. "Go ahead and start without me. I'll catch up!"

Jeremy groaned. He had heard this routine too many times.

"Dogs are a lot of work," Mr. Bluett began. "Having a dog is almost like having—"

"—a baby in the house," finished Mrs. Bluett as she came into the room. She smiled at her husband. "I told you I'd catch up."

Mr. Bluett nodded. "And nobody's home all day," he said.

"A dog needs company," Mrs. Bluett explained.

"Besides, dogs are expensive," Mr. Bluett said.

"Not this one," Robin said. "This one is free."

Jeremy knew the answer to that. He wondered why Robin kept trying.

"But we'd still have to pay for food and shots and . . ."

"I've got money," Robin said. "I can pay."

Mr. Bluett shook his head. "You haven't got enough," he said.

"And even if you did, it wouldn't matter," Mrs. Bluett said. "It's just not fair to leave a dog alone all day."

"How about a cat?" Robin asked.

Nobody bothered to answer that. They all knew—and they all knew Robin knew—that Mr. Bluett was allergic to cats.

"But I *need* a pet," Robin said softly. "I really do."

"I know, honey." Mrs. Bluett put her arm around Robin. "That's why we suggested fish."

"Fish don't mind being left alone all day," Mr. Bluett said.

"And they're not so expensive," Mrs. Bluett said.

Jeremy expected Robin to pick up the Wish Book and start pricing fish tanks again. But she surprised him.

"Fish are dumb," she said.

Of course, she was right. Fish had to be the most boring animals in the world. Squirrel had a whole tankful of tropical fish, and all they did was swim around in circles. For excitement, sometimes they opened and closed their mouths.

From the looks on his parents' faces, Jeremy could tell they knew fish were dumb, too.

"I want an animal with *fur*," Robin insisted.

Her parents looked at each other. Then the telephone rang, and they both jumped up to answer it.

"I'll get it," Mrs. Bluett said.

"No, I will," Mr. Bluett said.

Mrs. Bluett smiled at her husband. "You started this conversation about pets," she said. "I think you should end it."

She left the room, and Mr. Bluett sat down with a sigh. "So, Jeremy," he said, "do you think your friend will want to buy a classified ad?"

"I don't know," Jeremy said. "How much do they cost?"

"A dollar eighty-five a line," Mr. Bluett said, "with a three-line minimum."

Jeremy sighed. If he had that kind of money, he wouldn't be so worried about his school debt.

"Do you think you could get a free ad for him?"

Mr. Bluett shook his head. "I just work for the newspaper," he said. "I don't own it."

Jeremy looked back at the ad for the free beagle. Then he looked at the ad for the beagle that cost $250.

"Maybe we could get the free beagle for just a day," he suggested. "We could get him tomorrow, when everybody is home."

"A beagle?" Robin asked. "Tomorrow?"

"Calm down," Mr. Bluett said. "We're not getting a dog for just one day. What would we do with him on Monday?"

"We could sell him," Jeremy said. For $250, he thought.

"You're a real animal-lover, aren't you?" his father said.

Robin looked disgusted. "I want an animal I can *keep*," she said.

Mrs. Bluett came back to the family room with a puzzled look on her face.

"Are we having some kind of trouble that I don't know about?" she asked.

"I don't know," Mr. Bluett said. "Are we?"

"That was Evelyn Gerard on the phone," Mrs. Bluett said. "She says she thinks it's wonderful the way Jeremy and Robin are pitching in to help with our difficulties. She wants to know if there's anything she can do to help."

"What difficulties?" Mr. Bluett asked.

Mrs. Bluett looked at Jeremy and Robin. "Do you know anything about this?" she asked.

They both shook their heads.

"I shoveled her walk today," Robin said. "She paid me ten dollars."

"Ten dollars!" her father said. "For that little walk?"

"I think she felt sorry for me," Robin said. "It was pretty cold."

Jeremy wondered why no one had felt sorry for him when he was taking his violin door-to-door. He'd been cold, too.

"But she said *Jeremy* was pitching in, too," Mrs. Bluett said, looking even more puzzled.

"I tried to sell her something," Jeremy said, "but she didn't buy it."

"What did you try to sell?" his mother asked.

"Uh . . . something I don't need anymore."

"What?"

"My violin," he said softly.

"*Your violin?*" His mother gasped.

"I don't use it anymore," Jeremy said. "And, besides, it's too small for me. You said so yourself."

"And what," his mother asked, in an even voice, "did you tell Mrs. Gerard?"

"I just said that I needed money," Jeremy said, "and you couldn't give it to me."

"I'd better call her back and straighten this out before she arranges a telethon for us." Mrs. Bluett started to go, but stopped with a horrible thought: "You didn't sell your violin to somebody else, did you?"

"No," Jeremy said. "Nobody wanted it."

"You can be thankful for that," she said. "I want you to save that violin for your grandchildren."

"Jeremy's going to have grandchildren?" Robin looked at him, incredulous.

"If he lives long enough," said his mother, on her way back to the phone in the kitchen.

Mr. Bluett watched her leave, then turned to Jeremy. "I don't suppose your friend wants to advertise a violin in the newspaper?"

Jeremy didn't say anything.

"How much is he asking?"

"Two hundred dollars," Jeremy said.

His father whistled. "I asked at a music store, and they offered only forty bucks for it."

Jeremy looked at him in surprise. "*You* were going to sell it?"

"Not after I heard forty bucks. It didn't seem worth mentioning to your mom."

Jeremy didn't know why not. Forty dollars was a lot of money. He could pay back the school, buy some Big Bubba, a few football helmets, and maybe a poster or two. He probably couldn't afford the World Series, but maybe he could get a ticket to a regular-season game.

"Where is this music store?" Jeremy asked.

"Forget it," his father said. "Maybe your grandchildren would forgive you, but your mother wouldn't."

"Tell me, Mr. Bluett," the reporter says, "did your family pitch in and help you make your first million dollars?"

"No," Jeremy says. "They didn't help a bit."

The reporter shakes his head. "I'm amazed," he says.

Jeremy nods sadly. "So was I."

7

*J*eremy took *The Advocate-Journal* up to his room that night so he could study the classifieds. Maybe there was something else—something besides a beagle— that he could get for free and sell to somebody else.

He saw lots of ads for free cats and kittens. Maybe he could sell the kittens so quickly that Mr. Bluett's allergies wouldn't even know they were there. But then he remembered how much trouble Carl Castaldi had had giving away a litter of kittens in the third grade. Cats and kittens could be even harder to sell than a violin.

Then he saw another ad:

> FERTILE GERBILS free with
> cage. Call Basil at 555-3754.

Fertile gerbils. They would have babies. And Jeremy could sell them.

He wondered how much people would pay for a baby gerbil. He looked quickly through the rest of the pet ads, but nobody else was offering gerbils. They must be rare—maybe even worth a lot of money.

He thought of Eloise, the gerbil that Mrs. Kramer kept in the fourth grade classroom at Dolley Madison. Everybody liked Eloise. He bet every kid in school would like to have his own Eloise.

Heck, every kid in the country would like to have his own Eloise. Jeremy could run a gerbil farm right here in his room, and a steady stream of cars with out-of-state license plates would come, bringing kids to buy his gerbils. He might even start a mail order business.

But first he needed the fertile gerbils. And something told him that his mother wasn't going to be crazy about having a gerbil farm in her house. He would need help in getting her approval.

He went to Robin's room and knocked on the door.

"Robin?" He spoke softly, so his parents wouldn't hear.

There was no answer, so he opened the door. The only light in the room came from a Wonder Woman night-light. Robin's eyes were closed, and she was breathing deeply.

Jeremy walked over to her bed.

"Robin!" he said.

"Snarfle," she mumbled, and turned over.

He shook her shoulder. "Robin!" he said. "Robin!"

She rubbed her eyes.

"Robin!" he said. "Are you awake?"

She kept rubbing her eyes and snarfling.

"Look," he said. "Here's a pet with fur."

Instantly she was awake, looking around. "Where?"

Jeremy held up the newspaper. "It's an ad for free gerbils."

"Gerbils!" she squealed. "Free gerbils!"

Their parents came running.

"What happened?" Mr. Bluett said. "We heard someone scream!"

"Jeremy found some gerbils," Robin said.

"Where?" Mrs. Bluett pulled the hem of her nightgown around her ankles and looked uneasily at the floor.

"They're not here," Jeremy assured her. "I just found an ad in the newspaper."

"They're free," Robin said.

"And you woke up Robin to tell her about it?" Mrs. Bluett asked.

"She was practically awake anyway," Jeremy said.

"Practically," Mr. Bluett said.

"I was," Robin insisted. "I was just lying here thinking how nice it would be to have some gerbils of my own."

"Sure," Mr. Bluett said. "And I was just lying there thinking how nice it would be to have a quiet night with my wife."

"I really do want gerbils," Robin insisted.

"And I really want a quiet night with my wife," her father said. "We'll talk about gerbils in the morning."

In the morning Robin led the way into their parents' bedroom. Jeremy stood by the door and watched her go to work. She crawled into bed between her parents.

"Good morning, Mommy," Robin purred. "Good morning, Daddy."

"Good morning, sweetheart," Mrs. Bluett said.

Mr. Bluett groaned. "What time is it?"

"It's time to decide about the gerbils," Robin said in her purring voice. "Can we get them?"

Mr. Bluett groaned again.

"Can we?"

Mr. Bluett opened his eyes to look at Robin, then Jeremy. "Oh no," he said. "It's a full-force frontal assault."

"Gerbils don't mind being left alone all day," Jeremy said.

"And they're not expensive," Robin said.

"I don't know," Mrs. Bluett said, propping her head up with her elbow. "Aren't gerbils just like mice?"

"Sort of," Mr. Bluett said. "A gerbil is kind of a cross between a mouse and a rat."

"A rat!" Mrs. Bluett gasped and fell back on her pillow.

"A little rat," her husband said.

"I don't think we want *a little rat* running around the house," Mrs. Bluett said.

"Oh, please!" Robin cried and snuggled closer to her mother. "Pretty please!"

"They don't run around the house," Jeremy told his mother. "Our class had one last year, and we kept her in a cage."

He didn't mention the three days that Eloise had been missing. Instead, he told her what gerbils could do. "They run around on a little wheel," he said, "and you can build mazes for them to run through."

"Mazes?" Mrs. Bluett perked up at the sound of something educational.

"Of course, we'd have to buy a cage," Mr. Bluett said.

"No," Jeremy said. "The ad says the cage is free, too."

"Let me see that ad." Mr. Bluett propped a pillow behind his head and took the newspaper from Jeremy.

"Who would clean the cage?" Mrs. Bluett asked.

"I would!" Robin cried.

Mrs. Bluett looked at Jeremy.

"I'd help her," he said.

"Hold it," Mr. Bluett said. "The ad says these gerbils are *fertile*."

Mrs. Bluett gasped again. "Fertile!"

Robin looked worried. "Is that bad?"

"It means they can have babies," Jeremy told her.

"Babies!" she squealed.

"Litters," Mrs. Bluett said, shaking her head. "I'm not going to have litters of rats all over the house. That's too much to ask."

"It would be a great way to learn about sex," Jeremy said.

His parents both looked at him.

"I mean, reproduction," Jeremy said.

"Huh," his father said.

But Jeremy saw interest in his mother's eyes, so he kept talking. "It would be sort of like living on a farm," he said. "We could witness the miracle of birth."

Mrs. Bluett smiled—one of her listening-to-the-orchestra smiles—and Jeremy felt a flutter of hope.

"But what would we do with the babies?" she asked.

"Keep them!" Robin cried, and Mrs. Bluett's smile disappeared.

Jeremy moved in quickly to repair the damage. "I could sell them," he said.

"Nobody will buy a gerbil," Mrs. Bluett said. "Look, this man is giving them away."

"Somebody was giving away a beagle, too," Jeremy pointed out. "And somebody else was selling one for two hundred and fifty dollars."

"Beagles are different," his mother said. "Nobody's going to buy a gerbil."

"Oh, lots of people will," Jeremy said. "They're very popular pets."

Robin nodded. "Pet stores are full of them," she said.

"Probably because nobody will buy them," Mr. Bluett said.

Jeremy ignored his father and concentrated on his mother. "The stores have to get gerbils from somewhere," he said. "I could be their supplier." He could do that at first, before the out-of-state license plates started coming.

Mrs. Bluett looked at her husband.

"Maybe he could *give* gerbils to a pet store," Mr. Bluett conceded. "I wouldn't count on selling them."

"Can we get them?" Robin asked. "Can we?"

Mrs. Bluett hesitated. "I don't know," she said. "I just keep thinking of *litters*."

"You mean the miracle of birth," Jeremy said.

"I want *fur*," purred Robin, snuggling closer to her mother. "Gerbils are furry."

"We would have to call a pet store," Mrs. Bluett said, "to make sure they'd take any extra babies."

Jeremy ran for the telephone.

8

*J*eremy called every pet store in the yellow pages, but nobody answered.

"It's Sunday morning," Mr. Bluett reminded him. "They probably don't open until ten o'clock or maybe noon."

Jeremy knew the family would be at church at ten o'clock.

"We'd better call Basil now," he said, "and let him know we're interested."

"Who's Basil?" his mother asked.

"The guy who's giving away the gerbils," Jeremy reminded her.

"Nobody's calling Basil until we're sure a pet store will take the babies," his mother said.

"But somebody else might get the free gerbils," Jeremy warned.

"What an awful thought," Mrs. Bluett said.

As soon as they got home from church, Jeremy ran inside and started dialing again. At 11:58 a woman answered the phone at Petland.

"I'm sorry," she said. "We have more gerbils than we can handle right now. You might try Buckeye Pets, though. They have a large snake collection."

Jeremy didn't know what snakes had to do with gerbils, but he called Buckeye Pets anyway. By now it was three minutes after noon, and a man answered.

"Sure," he said, "I'll take any extra gerbils."

"How much will you pay for them?"

"*Pay* for them?" The man laughed. "Listen, kid, I'll be doing you a favor to take them off your hands."

Jeremy hoped this guy would come to him for a job on his gerbil farm. Jeremy would turn him down flat.

His mother got on the phone.

"Yes," she said. "I understand . . . No, money isn't important . . . I just want to make sure we're not stuck with a dozen rodents."

When Mrs. Bluett hung up, she agreed to call the number in the ad.

Jeremy and Robin both kept their fingers crossed while she dialed the number. It must have worked, because Basil said he still had the gerbils. He said he was going to a basketball game today, though, and the Bluetts couldn't get the gerbils until Monday.

"I don't mind waiting," Mrs. Bluett said.

The next day Kevin wore a Cincinnati Reds jacket to school. It had two thin white stripes around the sleeves and collar, and it said *Reds* on the back.

"It's the most comfortable jacket I've ever worn," Kevin said, showing off its soft quilted lining.

Jeremy already knew how comfortable a Reds jacket was because he had tried one on at Sears in the fall. He had wanted to buy it, but Mrs. Bluett had said no, it was too expensive. She said maybe he could buy a Reds jacket when he stopped growing.

But maybe he could buy one sooner, now that he was starting his own business.

"I'm going to buy a Reds jacket, too," Jeremy said.

"But, Germy, I thought your mom said they were too expensive," Squirrel said.

"I'm going to pay for it myself," Jeremy said.

Kevin laughed.

"I'm starting a gerbil farm," Jeremy said. "I'm going to make lots of money."

Kevin laughed again, but Squirrel was interested.

"A gerbil farm?" he asked. "Will you have to move to the country?"

"No," Jeremy said. "I'm going to raise gerbils in my room and sell them."

Kevin stopped laughing, but he still looked skeptical. "Who's going to buy them?"

"Kids," Jeremy said.

"What kids?" Kevin asked.

"All kinds of kids," Jeremy said. "Everybody'll want one."

"I won't," said Kevin.

"But lots of other kids will," Squirrel said loyally.

Kevin looked Squirrel in the eye. "Will you buy a gerbil from Germy?" he asked.

Squirrel didn't blink. "Sure," he said. "I'll be his first customer."

Kevin snorted and walked away.

"You don't have to buy a gerbil," Jeremy told Squirrel. "I'll give you one—for free."

∽

Mr. Bluett brought the gerbils home with him in a wire cage that afternoon. One sat in the middle of the cage, watchful. The other ran frantically on a stationary wheel.

Mrs. Bluett looked in the cage just once.

"Oh," she said weakly. "They *do* look like little rats." She went over to the couch and sat down.

But Robin was excited. "Aren't they cute?" she cried as she flipped open the cage and reached inside.

"Take it easy," her father said. "Basil thinks the female is pregnant."

Mrs. Bluett moaned.

"Which one is she?" Robin asked.

"It's hard to tell," her father said. "I think she's the quiet one. Basil called her Big Mama."

Jeremy liked the name.

"What's the boy gerbil called?" Robin asked.

"Uh, he didn't say."

Jeremy looked at his father. Mr. Bluett obviously knew the male gerbil's name but didn't want to say it.

"Let's call him Charlie," Robin said.

"Perfect." Mr. Bluett looked relieved. "Charlie's a great name."

"What's this?" Robin asked, tapping a clear plastic bottle that hung from the side of the cage.

"It's a water bottle," her father said. "You'll have to make sure they have plenty of water all the time, and you'll have to feed them once a day." He held up an almost empty paper bag with RODENT FOOD printed on the side.

45

"We'd better go to the pet store and buy more of this stuff."

Jeremy and Robin nodded.

"Now," Mr. Bluett said, "where will we keep them?"

"In the cage," his wife said from the couch. "Definitely in the cage."

"In my room!" Robin cried. "In my room!"

"I think we should keep them in *my* room," Jeremy said. "After all, I'm the breeder."

"The what?" Everyone looked at him.

"I'm the one who's going to find homes for the babies," he explained.

"Maybe we could keep one in Jeremy's room and one in mine," Robin suggested.

"They have to stay in their cage," Mrs. Bluett said firmly.

"I could buy another cage with my snow shoveling money," Robin offered.

"No," Jeremy said. "Charlie and Big Mama have to be together if we want them to make babies."

"Oh." Robin's eyes grew wide. "That's right."

"Let's flip a coin," Mr. Bluett said, taking a quarter from his pocket. "The winner gets to keep Charlie and Big Mama for the first week. After that, you take turns."

Robin called heads, but it came up tails.

Jeremy smiled generously at her. "You can carry their food," he said, taking the cage from his father.

"It isn't fair," Robin said. "I meant to call tails, but I got mixed up."

"Be a good sport, Robin," her father said. "You'll have your turn next week."

Robin pouted, but she followed Jeremy up the stairs.

"Oh, and one more thing," Mr. Bluett called after them. "Basil said to give them something to chew—paper, cardboard, anything. If they don't have something to chew, they'll probably start chewing on their cage, and then . . ." He glanced at his wife. ". . . they might escape."

Mrs. Bluett moaned.

9

Jeremy took the cage into his room and set it on his desk. Then he bent down so he could see Big Mama's belly. She looked a little chubby, but Jeremy couldn't tell whether she was pregnant or just fat.

"Oooh!" Robin purred. "Aren't they cute?" She unlatched the lid and put her hand inside the cage. Charlie scampered around the cage, but Big Mama approached Robin's hand cautiously and sniffed it.

"What are you doing?" Jeremy asked.

"Letting her sniff me," Robin said. "I want her to know I'm her friend."

"You'd better keep your eye on Char—"

But it was too late. Charlie had scampered right up the wire cage and taken a running leap out of the open top.

Too late, Robin pulled out her hand and slammed the lid shut.

"Now look what you've done," Jeremy said.

"Where'd he go?" Robin asked.

"Under the bed, I think."

They both looked under the bed.

"What a mess," Robin said, poking at an empty Cheetos bag. "We'll never find him here."

Charlie emerged from an old tennis shoe and scampered toward the closet. Robin lunged at him, but missed.

"Geez, he's fast," Jeremy said.

"We'll never catch him," Robin said, looking at the dirty clothes and papers piled on the closet floor. "This is worse than under your bed."

"We'll just have to wait him out," Jeremy said. "That's what we did when our class gerbil got loose last year."

"How long did it take to catch him?"

"It was a her, and it took three days."

"*Three days?*" Robin groaned.

Jeremy didn't like the idea, either. The more he thought about it, the more he thought his mother was right. Charlie looked like a rat.

They heard the rustle of cellophane. Then they heard the sound of munching.

"Is there another Cheetos bag in there?" Robin asked. "With some crumbs left?"

Jeremy shrugged. "Maybe."

There was a knock on the door. Robin and Jeremy looked at each other.

Mrs. Bluett opened the door. "Dinner'll be ready in five minutes. You'd better get down there and set the table."

"Okay," Jeremy said, hoping she'd leave and shut the door before Charlie took off again.

But she didn't leave. Instead, she came in and sat on Jeremy's bed.

"I also want to talk to you about the . . . uh . . . rodents," she said. "To be honest with you, I'm sorry I ever agreed to have the things in the house."

Jeremy moved over to shut the door. Robin positioned herself in front of the closet.

"But what's done is done," their mother said. "So I'll live with them, under one condition: You *must* keep them in the cage. Do you understand?"

Jeremy and Robin nodded.

Something rustled in the closet, and Jeremy coughed to cover the noise.

"Are you coming down with something?" his mother asked.

Jeremy shook his head. But there was another rustle, and he coughed again. Robin started coughing, too.

"I think I'll set the table myself," Mrs. Bluett said. "I don't want you two spreading germs."

They both stopped coughing when she left.

Something rustled again. Jeremy peered over the mess in his closet. He spotted something shiny between a soccer shin guard and a baseball card album. Another rustle, and the shiny thing moved slightly. It must be a Cheetos bag, with Charlie inside.

He hesitated, for just a minute. But he knew he had to get Charlie out of his closet and back in the cage.

"Stand back!" he yelled as he swept down on the bag and scooped it up. Sure enough, Charlie was inside, scampering frantically back and forth among the orange crumbs. Jeremy held the top of the bag tightly, so he couldn't escape.

"He needs air!" Robin cried.

"Then open the cage!"

When she lifted the lid, Jeremy dumped Charlie and the crumbs into the cage. Big Mama ran over to Charlie and sniffed him.

Jeremy shut the lid quickly and plopped a dictionary on top.

Robin ran to her room and back again.

"Open the cage!" she said.

Open the cage? She had to be kidding.

"I want to give them some old valentines." She held up a batch of red and white cards from her class party.

Jeremy still didn't open the cage.

"Jeremeee!" she cried. "If we don't give them something to chew on, they might chew their way out of the cage and get *really* lost!"

Jeremy opened the cage, and Robin dropped in two valentines.

"There you go," she cooed. "One for each of you."

The gerbils pounced on the valentines and began shredding them with their teeth. Jeremy snapped the lid shut and put the dictionary on top again.

Robin looked at him. "You're scared of them, aren't you?"

Jeremy laughed heartily. "Me? Scared? Don't be silly!"

"Then touch one of them."

Jeremy looked at the rodents slicing through the valentines with their teeth. "I don't feel like it right now."

Robin nodded. "You're scared."

"I just caught Charlie," Jeremy said. "That proves I'm not scared."

"But you didn't *touch* Charlie," Robin pointed out. "You just held the bag he was in." She smiled. "Face it, Jeremy. You're scared of gerbils."

Jeremy laughed again, even more heartily.

After dinner Mr. Bluett took Jeremy and Robin to Buck-eye Pets. While their father paid for the cedar chips and rodent food, they looked at clear plastic cages with gerbil-sized tunnels leading to staircases and turrets.

"Oh," Robin breathed. "How beautiful!"

Jeremy checked the price tag. The beautiful plastic cage cost forty-eight dollars. Even if Jeremy had that kind of money, he wouldn't spend it on a couple of rodents.

But Robin might. "Maybe I could buy this with my snow shoveling money," she said.

Jeremy knew it would take a few years for Robin to make a decision like that, so he went to check on the price of baby gerbils.

They cost five dollars each.

"How many babies are in a litter?" he asked a woman cleaning the cages.

"It varies," she said. "Usually six or eight."

Eight baby gerbils! Forty dollars!

"And how often do they have babies?"

"That varies, too," she said. "If you keep the male and female together, they'll usually have a litter every four to six weeks."

That was about once a month. And there were twelve months in a year.

Twelve times forty was forty-eight. Wait, that wasn't right. Twelve times forty was 480.

Four hundred and eighty dollars! And this was just the beginning.

❧

The reporter touches the green and white wallpaper. "Gee, Mr. Bluett," he says. "This almost looks real."

"It is," Jeremy tells him. "The whole building is papered with one-hundred dollar bills."

❧

That night Jeremy lay awake in his darkened room and listened to the gerbils. He heard scratching and chewing, then the wheel squeaking. Charlie was probably going for a spin.

Jeremy put a pillow over his head, but he could still hear them. Finally he flipped on the light.

"Don't you guys know what time it is?" he asked. The gerbils didn't even look at him.

He went over to their cage and rattled the lid. "Hey!" he said. "Be quiet in there!"

Charlie stopped running on the wheel, and Big Mama stopped chewing on her valentine. They sat on their hind legs and looked at him.

He looked back.

Imagine Robin thinking he was scared of a couple of little gerbils.

Then why couldn't he touch them?

He could touch them. He just didn't feel like it.

Why not?

It was no big deal. He'd just stick his hand in the cage and let them sniff it, just like Robin had done.

No, that would be stupid. If they could chew their way out of a cage, who knows what they could do with a hand? He should just reach into the cage quickly, touch a gerbil, and get his hand out of there.

Jeremy lifted the lid. He decided to aim for Big Mama. And he'd better do it now, before Charlie took another running leap.

He shut his eyes, reached down, and touched the tip

of Big Mama's tail as she scampered away. He quickly pulled his hand out of the cage and slammed the lid shut.

There. That proved he wasn't afraid.

But it didn't quiet the gerbils. As soon as he turned off the light, they started scratching, sniffing, chewing, and running on the wheel again.

Jeremy thought about taking the gerbils to Robin's room so they could scratch, sniff, chew, and run in her ear all night. But if he did that, Robin would say he was scared.

He flipped on the light again and looked inside the cage. Big Mama was nearly finished with her valentine. She'd made a little pile of red and white scraps in the corner of the cage. It looked like a nest.

A nest for her five-dollar babies.

10

Jeremy awoke to high-pitched squealing on Wednesday morning. At first he thought the disc jockey on his clock radio had swallowed some helium and was talking funny. Then he noticed that the squealing came from the gerbil cage.

When he looked in the cage, he saw Big Mama lying in the valentine nest with a bunch of tiny pink pencil erasers around her. In the center of the cage, Charlie was standing on his hind legs, twitching his tail.

One of the erasers moved.

"Holy cow!" Jeremy yelled. "Big Mama did it!"

Robin came running.

"What are those things?" she asked when she looked inside the cage.

"Those," Jeremy said proudly, "are baby gerbils."

"They are?" Robin looked more closely. "Oooh! They are!" She flipped the lid open and started to reach inside.

"Leave them alone!" Jeremy said. "You might squish them."

"I wouldn't do that," Robin said. "I was going to be very, very gentle." But she took her hand out of the cage.

He counted at least six babies. Thirty dollars.

"Why don't they have any hair?" Robin asked. "And why don't they open their eyes?"

"They just got here," Jeremy said. "Give them time."

"Who just got here?" Mrs. Bluett asked from the doorway. "And what's that funny noise?"

"Big Mama had her babies!" Robin announced.

"Really?" Mrs. Bluett came in and looked inside the cage. "Goodness, they don't have any hair, do they?"

Mr. Bluett stopped in the hall and patted the bald spot on top of his head. "Who doesn't have any hair?"

"The baby gerbils," Robin said. "Big Mama just had them."

"No kidding?" Mr. Bluett came in and looked in the cage, too. "When did this happen?"

"I don't know," Jeremy said. "They were here when I woke up."

Mr. Bluett looked at Jeremy. "So you missed the miracle of birth."

Jeremy didn't care. The five-dollar gerbils were here.

"How many are there?" his mother asked.

"I've counted six so far," Jeremy said, "but it's hard to tell with Big Mama right there. We'll be able to see better when she moves."

Robin started to rattle the cage, but Mrs. Bluett stopped her.

"Let the poor thing rest," she said. "She must be exhausted."

Jeremy and Robin looked at their mother. Was she softening toward Big Mama, now that she'd had babies?

"Charlie looks pooped, too," their father said. "Even his tail is twitching."

"I don't know why *he's* tired," Mrs. Bluett said. "Big Mama's the one who did all the work."

"But he had to keep her spirits up," Mr. Bluett said. "That can be tough."

Jeremy didn't care how Big Mama and Charlie felt. The important thing was the thirty dollars squealing in their nest.

&

"Exactly how did you make your first million, Mr. Bluett?" the reporter asks.

"I was in the breeding business."

"Horses?"

"No, gerbils."

"Oh, are you the one who made gerbils so popular?"

Jeremy smiles. "My little business just grew and grew until gerbils were the most popular pets in the country. Why, you hardly ever see a dog anymore."

"A dog?" The young reporter laughs. "Do you mean people used to keep dogs as pets?"

"Some people did," Jeremy says. "Now everyone has a gerbil."

The reporter nods. "I like my gerbil better than most people I know."

&

"Big Mama had her babies," Jeremy told Squirrel in the school parking lot.

"Yeah?" Squirrel said. "When do I get mine?"

"I don't know," Jeremy said. "They're pretty little right now."

"I want the biggest one," Squirrel said. "I'm going to name him Bruno."

Michael Taylor came up. "Who's Bruno?" he asked.

"My new gerbil," Squirrel said. "Germy's gerbils just had babies, and I'm going to get the biggest one."

Michael looked at Jeremy. "Baby gerbils?" he said. "Can I have one, too?"

"They cost five dollars each," Jeremy said.

"Five dollars?" Michael said. "I'll have to think about it."

Other kids didn't hesitate. By lunchtime, seventeen kids had placed orders for the five-dollar babies. Jeremy wondered if there were any way he could hurry along the next litter.

A few kids balked at the price.

"Five dollars is pretty expensive," said David Jones.

"That's what you'd pay at Buckeye Pets," Jeremy said.

"But you don't have any overhead," Kevin Johansen said.

"Overhead?"

"You don't have to pay employees or deal with shoplifters," Kevin explained. He knew a lot about small businesses because of the convenience stores on his father's truck route. "That's why I sold the Twinkies for less than you'd pay in a store."

"Your Twinkies were also stale," Squirrel said. "There's nothing wrong with Germy's gerbils. They're probably better than the ones you'd buy in a store. Right, Germy?"

"Right." Jeremy grinned at Squirrel.

"And I get Bruno for free," Squirrel reminded him.

Jeremy nodded. The thirty dollars dropped to twenty-five, but a promise was a promise.

Mrs. Bluett still seemed interested in the gerbils that afternoon. As soon as they got home, she went upstairs with Jeremy and Robin to check on the gerbil family.

Charlie was chasing Big Mama around the cage.

"What are they doing?" Robin asked.

"It looks like Charlie wants a bigger family," Mrs. Bluett said. "I wonder if we should take him out of there, so Big Mama and her babies can get some rest."

Jeremy thought of the seventeen orders for baby gerbils. "No," he said. "With all those babies, Big Mama probably needs his help."

"He doesn't look very helpful right now," Mrs. Bluett said.

"We don't have another cage," Jeremy reminded her.

Mrs. Bluett nodded. The babies might be interesting, but she still didn't want any gerbils loose in her house.

With Big Mama on the run, Jeremy had a clear view of the nest. He counted five pink babies.

"Hey!" he said. "There are supposed to be six babies."

"Maybe you counted wrong this morning," his mother said.

"No, I'm sure there were six," Jeremy said. "I even thought there might be more."

"Oh, my poor baby!" Robin cried.

Jeremy felt like crying, too. With one less baby, he was down to twenty dollars.

"What happened?" Robin wailed. "What happened to my baby?"

They all looked at Charlie suspiciously.

11

"*I* don't think you should blame Charlie," Mr. Bluett said when they told him at dinner about the missing baby gerbil. "I talked to a guy at work who used to raise gerbils. He said the mother gerbil sometimes eats a baby if she thinks there's something wrong with it."

"Big Mama wouldn't do that!" Robin said. "She loves her babies!"

"But maybe that's her way of protecting the rest of the litter," Mrs. Bluett said.

Jeremy looked at his mother in surprise.

So did Robin. "Would you eat me just to protect Jeremy?" she asked.

Mrs. Bluett laughed. "Of course not. But I'm not a gerbil."

"And we can all be thankful for that," her husband said.

"Do you think Big Mama will eat any more?" Jeremy asked. Robin moaned.

"Probably not," Mr. Bluett said. "She probably gave them all the once-over and decided the others are fine."

Jeremy hoped so. He couldn't afford to lose any more five-dollar babies.

"Let's look at the bright side," Mrs. Bluett said, twirling spaghetti around her fork. "We have one less baby gerbil to find a home for."

"But that's not a problem," Jeremy said. "I've already got seventeen orders for baby gerbils."

His parents looked at him. "Seventeen?"

"Actually eighteen, if you count Squirrel."

"Why wouldn't you count your best friend?" his mother asked.

"He's not paying for his."

"The others are paying?" his father asked. "How much?"

"Five dollars," Jeremy said quietly. He didn't want to make business sound too good. Robin might claim part of it.

She didn't say anything, though, even when Mr. Bluett whistled and Mrs. Bluett shook her head.

"Five dollars!" Mrs. Bluett said. "Where do kids get that kind of money?"

"From their parents." Jeremy smiled at her. "They all have nice parents—and big allowances."

"Do these nice parents know their kids are buying gerbils?" Mrs. Bluett asked.

"I don't know," Jeremy said.

"Well, you'd better find out," she said. "I'm not letting anyone take a gerbil out of this house until I talk to his parents."

"Why?"

"I want to make sure they know what they're getting into," Mrs. Bluett said. "Some people don't like the idea of rodents in the house."

"And we don't want to be run out of town," Mr. Bluett said.

❧

After dinner Mr. Bluett went upstairs with Jeremy to check on the gerbils. Charlie had settled down now, and Big Mama lay in the nest, with the pink babies huddled around her belly.

Jeremy realized the babies were sucking milk from Big Mama, right in front of his father.

But Mr. Bluett didn't act embarrassed.

"She's nursing them," he said matter-of-factly, and Jeremy nodded, as if mothers nursed their babies in his bedroom all the time.

But he wondered how many nipples Big Mama had, and why he hadn't noticed them before.

"I have to admit I'm a little surprised you're so interested in these gerbils," Mr. Bluett said. "I can understand Robin, but you've never been a big animal-lover."

"I need the money."

"I know you do," his father said. "But there are other, surer ways of making money. If you spent just one afternoon shoveling sidewalks, for instance, you could pay off the school right away."

"But I don't *like* shoveling sidewalks," Jeremy said. "And I want to make more money than that."

Mr. Bluett nodded, and Jeremy knew he understood. Mr. Bluett always said it was important to think big.

"How much money do you think you'll make?" he asked.

"Lots," Jeremy said. He thought about telling his father about the out-of-state license plates and the World Series tickets. "Of course, it will take some time to get started."

Mr. Bluett nodded again, and they both watched the young business growing in the nest.

The babies continued to suckle, even after Jeremy's father left. Finally Big Mama shook them off and left the nest. One baby, with his eyes still shut, climbed out of the valentine nest and tried to follow her.

Big Mama picked him up with her teeth. For a moment Jeremy was afraid she was going to eat this baby, too, but she just carried him back to the nest and set him down. The baby crawled out again, and Big Mama carried him back again.

That one must be Bruno, Jeremy thought.

"Hey, Robin!" he called. "Come see this!"

Robin didn't come.

"Hey, Robin!" He went to her room and knocked on the door. "Robin? Aren't you going to come watch the gerbils?"

"No."

Jeremy opened the door. "The babies are moving around now."

But Robin didn't care. "I don't think I'll ever play with Big Mama again," she said.

"Why not?"

"I don't think I can forgive her," Robin said. "She *ate* her baby."

A terrible thought came to Jeremy. Robin might never want to keep the noisy gerbil cage in her room at night. And she might never feed the gerbils or clean their cage, either.

"Maybe Big Mama didn't eat the baby," Jeremy said. "Maybe we counted wrong this morning."

Robin shook her head. "We counted right."

"Maybe Charlie did it."

"That's not much better," Robin said. "What kind of daddy would eat his own baby?"

"Look, Robin," Jeremy said, "we don't know what happened. Maybe the baby got real sick and died while we were at school today. Or maybe there was a terrible, tragic accident."

"Then where's the baby's body?"

"I don't know," Jeremy admitted. "Maybe Big Mama and Charlie buried their baby in a pile of shredded valentines. Or maybe the baby fell out of the cage and got lost in the junk in my room."

Robin looked thoughtful, and Jeremy plunged ahead.

"The point is," he said, "we don't know what happened. Maybe Big Mama is in there right now, struggling with her grief. Maybe what she really needs right now is a friend."

Robin hesitated for a moment. Then she nodded and followed Jeremy into his room to comfort Big Mama.

12

Jeremy got his allowance Friday afternoon.

"Don't forget your school debt," Mrs. Bluett said as she handed him the dollar bill.

Jeremy nodded. How could he forget the school debt when he had five baby gerbils squealing in his room?

He walked right past the football helmet machines at Findley's that afternoon. Instead, while his mother squeezed grapefruit, he bought a bag of Big Bubba bubble gum. Jeremy had once learned how to blow a bubble using seventeen pieces of Big Bubba, but he knew he could lose a talent like that if he didn't practice every once in a while.

With the tax, the Big Bubba cost ninety-seven cents, and the clerk gave Jeremy three cents in change. Right next to the cash register was a can with a picture of a little girl struggling with crutches. "Please help me walk!" cried the words next to her.

What could Jeremy do? He dropped his three cents into the can, and the little girl smiled gratefully.

Robin marched into his room Sunday morning. "Sunday is the beginning of a new week," she announced.

"So?"

"This is my week to have the gerbils."

Jeremy didn't want to appear too eager. "Oh gee," he said. "Are you sure you want them?"

"Of course I'm sure," Robin said. "Now hand them over."

Mrs. Bluett sniffed the cage as Jeremy carried it to Robin's room.

"You should clean that thing," she said.

"I don't think we should disturb the babies," Jeremy said. Besides, who cared how the cage smelled, as long as it was in Robin's room?

Squirrel came over that afternoon to see the gerbils. Jeremy took him up to Robin's room, where Big Mama was lying on her side with the pink babies huddled around her belly.

"Geez Louise," Squirrel said. "What's going on?"

"Big Mama's feeding her babies," Jeremy said, with a straight face. "She does it all the time."

Squirrel kept a straight face, too. "How many nipples does she have?" he asked.

"Enough."

One of the babies left Big Mama and started crawling out of the nest.

"Look, " Jeremy said. "That's Bruno."

Squirrel grinned. "He's adventurous."

The next day Squirrel told everyone at school about Bruno. "He's the best one in the litter," he said. "Germy picked him out for me."

"Have you picked one out for me, too?" David Jones asked.

"Well . . ."

"What does he look like?"

That was easy. All the babies looked alike.

"Right now he doesn't have any fur," Jeremy said. "He's pink, and his eyes are shut."

"When can I have him?" David asked.

"I don't know," Jeremy said. "He's still getting milk from his mother. It'll probably be another two or three weeks."

David looked disappointed. Two or three weeks was a long time to wait for a gerbil.

And it was a long time for Jeremy to wait for his money. Maybe he should ask for reservation deposits. The first four kids who paid him would get babies out of the first litter.

He announced his reservation policy on the playground at noon.

"How big does the deposit have to be?" David asked.

"Three dollars," Jeremy said.

"Three dollars!" Michael Taylor said. Other kids groaned, too.

"Okay, two," Jeremy said.

"Wait a minute," said Andrew Blaney. "Before I lay down my two bucks, I want to see what I'm getting."

Andrew Blaney was new at Dolley Madison this year, and Jeremy hadn't paid much attention to him, except to notice that he picked his nose a lot.

But other kids agreed with Andrew.

"Yeah," David said. "I want to see my gerbil before I make any deposit."

"Okay," Jeremy said. "You can come see them."

"When?" asked Andrew, sticking an index finger up his nose.

Jeremy watched, fascinated. Sometimes he picked his nose, too, but never when he thought people were looking.

"When?" Andrew asked again, with his finger still in his nose.

"Uh, this weekend," Jeremy said. He knew his parents wouldn't want a crowd of gerbil-shoppers trooping through their house after work on a weekday. "The first four people who lay down money will get the first four gerbils."

"You won't sell Bruno, will you?" Squirrel asked later.

"Don't worry," Jeremy said. "Bruno's yours."

"Even if they offer cash?"

"Even if they offer cash."

On the way to Mrs. Carlson's house that afternoon, Jeremy saw a black cloud rise over a nearby neighborhood.

"What's that?" he asked Squirrel.

"Air pollution," Squirrel said. "It's getting worse every day. My mom says it's going to kill us all someday."

They didn't talk anymore. They both tried to take in short, shallow breaths, so the air pollution wouldn't kill them any sooner than it had to.

Robin ran up behind them. "Do you see the fire?" she asked. "Look at that smoke!"

"That's not smoke." Jeremy whispered, so he wouldn't breathe in too much of the deadly air. "That's air pollution."

"Oh," Robin said. And she started taking shallow breaths, too.

Mrs. Bluett came to pick them up early.

"I heard about the fire on the radio," she told Mrs. Carlson. "They didn't say exactly where it was, but they said there were two kids trapped inside, and I . . ."

"Now, Sally," Mrs. Carlson said, "you know I'd never leave your kids inside a burning building."

"I know." His mother smiled, but Jeremy saw in her eyes that she had been frightened. It made him feel special.

"Jeremy said it was *air pollution*," Robin reported. "I tried to tell him it was a fire, but he said it was air pollution!"

Mrs. Bluett laughed, and that special feeling disappeared.

&

When Mr. Bluett came home, he knew all about the fire. He always knew what was going on in town because his office at *The Advocate-Journal* was right across the hall from the newsroom.

"A kid was playing with matches . . ." he began.

"Matches!" Mrs. Bluett turned to her children. "How many times have I told you never to play with matches?"

"We didn't start the fire," Jeremy said. "We weren't even there."

"And we don't play with matches," Robin said. "That's baby stuff."

"Do you mind if I tell the rest of the story?" Mr. Bluett asked.

"That's what we're waiting for," his wife said. "Did they ever get the kids out?"

Mr. Bluett nodded. "The family dog went in and rescued them."

"The dog!" Mrs. Bluett said.

"The dog!" Robin repeated proudly, as if the dog were hers.

"The kids are both in critical condition," Mr. Bluett said.

"How's the dog?" Robin asked.

"He's okay, but the cat died. She was trapped in the basement."

"Oh!" Robin's lips trembled, and a chill swept over Jeremy.

"But the dog saved the kids," Mr. Bluett said. "Once this story gets out, people'll probably flock to the animal shelter to pick up a free dog."

"Maybe we can get one, too," Robin said hopefully, and this time Mrs. Bluett looked thoughtful.

"We already have gerbils," Mr. Bluett reminded them.

"But they wouldn't save us in a fire," Robin pointed out.

"That's only fair," her father said. "I probably wouldn't go into a fire to save them, either."

"You wouldn't?" asked Robin, shocked.

Mrs. Bluett's thoughtful look vanished. "No, he wouldn't," she said. "And you wouldn't, either. No animal is worth risking your life over." She turned to her husband. "Was anyone else injured?"

"No, but the house is a total loss."

"That poor family." Mrs. Bluett shook her head.

"A lot of people will feel that way," Mr. Bluett said. "We'll probably run a special appeal in tomorrow's edition."

"A special appeal?" Jeremy asked.

"You know," his father said, "a story that tugs at the heartstrings and tells readers what they can do to help the family."

Mrs. Bluett nodded. "We should write a check," she said, "and we should find out how old the kids are. Maybe they can use some clothes or toys we've outgrown."

"And maybe we can give the kids a baby gerbil, too," Robin said. "That might help them forget about their cat."

Oh no, Jeremy thought. First he promised Squirrel a free

gerbil, and now these kids expected theirs free, too. Pretty soon he wasn't going to have any left to sell.

Immediately Jeremy felt guilty. These poor kids were in the hospital and had lost everything, even their cat. If a free gerbil would make them feel better, Jeremy wanted them to have it.

But Mrs. Bluett shook her head. "Those parents have enough problems," she said. "They don't need rodents."

13

The Advocate-Journal had a big front-page story about the fire the next day. There was even a picture of the fire chief hanging a medal around the dog's neck.

"If any dog ever deserved a little pomp and circumstance, that one did," Mrs. Bluett said, looking at the newspaper. "He's a real hero."

"He's been good for the paper, too," Mr. Bluett said. "We sold out at the newsstands this afternoon."

"Does that mean we can get a dog?" Robin asked.

"No," her father said, "it means that people like tragedies."

"Oh, Hank." Mrs. Bluett put down the newspaper.

"It's true. You should see the lobby of the newspaper office. People have donated furniture, appliances, bedding, clothes, toys, everything you can imagine."

Mrs. Bluett nodded. "Something like this frightens

everyone. I keep thinking, 'That could have been our house; those could have been our kids trapped inside.' "

"But it couldn't have been our dog running in to save us," Robin said, "because we don't have a dog."

Mrs. Bluett looked thoughtful. "I know."

"Sally," her husband said, "I thought we agreed about this dog business."

Mrs. Bluett smiled and patted his hand. "Don't worry," she said. "I'm not going to do anything foolish."

⌒

Mr. Bluett picked up Robin and Jeremy at Mrs. Carlson's house Thursday afternoon.

"Your mother called and said she would be late," he said.

Jeremy and Robin looked at each other. Their parents never called each other *your mother* or *your father* unless they were having an argument.

"I suppose we can go ahead and make dinner without your mother," Mr. Bluett said. He turned the car into Findley's. "I'll just stop here and pick up a few things."

Jeremy and Robin stayed in the car. It was best to keep a low profile when their parents were arguing.

When Mr. Bluett got back in the car, he was whistling. "I got some hot dogs and potato chips," he said. "How does that sound?"

"Great!" Jeremy said. His mother never bought hot dogs because of all the sodium nitrite and other junk in them. And to think they were having potato chips, too. He wondered what the special occasion was.

Then he remembered. The Argument.

"And I bought some Coke, too," Mr. Bluett said. "Yes, sir, it'll be a great supper tonight."

"Uh-oh," Robin said.

But they forgot all about the argument when their mother came home. She had a dog.

"A dog!" Robin fell to the floor beside the dog. "Can we keep him? Can we? Can we?"

Mrs. Bluett looked at her husband. "I think so," she said.

The dog had short legs and a belly that practically dragged on the floor, but he was still a dog. Suddenly Jeremy knew what the argument was about.

But Robin evidently didn't. "Oh!" she cried. "This is the happiest day of my life!"

Jeremy watched his parents watching each other.

"Our receptionist's mother-in-law died, and she inherited her old dog," Mrs. Bluett said. "She can't keep him in her apartment, so she was going to give him to the animal shelter. But then I thought, 'Why don't we take him?' "

"An interesting question," Mr. Bluett said.

"He won't be any trouble at all," his wife said. "He's an old dog, so he'll just sleep all day. And he's housebroken, too."

"Huh," Mr. Bluett said, eyeing the dog.

"You know they'd never find a home for such an old dog," Mrs. Bluett said. "They'd just have to put him to sleep."

"You mean *kill* him?" Robin cried, hugging the dog. "We wouldn't let that happen, would we?"

Mr. Bluett looked at his wife. "You're not playing fair," he said.

"What's his name?" Jeremy asked.

"George," his mother said, without taking her eyes off Mr. Bluett.

"George?" Mr. Bluett repeated. "That's not a dog's name."

"Well, it's this dog's name," his wife said. "And now we won't have to worry about burglars or fires or anything like that. George here will protect us."

Mr. Bluett looked at George's sagging belly. "I don't think he can climb the stairs."

"But he can bark," Mrs. Bluett said.

George stretched out on Robin's lap and fell asleep.

Mrs. Bluett didn't say anything about the hot dogs or the potato chips. But she pointed out that the Coke contained caffeine, which would keep everyone awake all night.

"Maybe we should give some to George," Mr. Bluett said. George was asleep under the kitchen table.

"Georgie needs his sleep," Robin said. "This has been a big day for him, getting a new family."

After dinner Mrs. Bluett took Robin to Buckeye Pets to buy some dog food and a leash. They also bought a rawhide bone, two squeaky toys, and a woolen dog coat.

"A dog coat?" Mr. Bluett said when they came home. "Don't you think this is getting a little out of hand?"

"I don't want Georgie to get cold," Robin said. "His belly drags in the snow."

"She paid for the coat with her own money," Mrs. Bluett explained.

Jeremy looked at the dog coat. It was fancy, with fur trim around the edges. Robin must have spent almost all of her money.

"What happened to your idea of saving until you have a hundred dollars? Or a thousand?" he asked Robin.

"Some things are more important than money," she said.

Robin carried George up the stairs to her room, and Jeremy went to bed early, too. He wanted to leave his parents alone so they would finish their argument.

Upstairs in his room, Jeremy could hear his father's voice rise and fall. He talked about united fronts and schedules and who's going to walk the dog during a blinding blizzard. His mother was loud sometimes, too. She talked about safety and companionship and childhood memories. And she said she would walk the dog herself during a blinding blizzard.

The voices went on and on. Finally there was a knock on Jeremy's door.

"Jeremy?" It was Robin.

"Come on in." He was glad she was there.

She came over to his bed and sat down. "This is because of Georgie, isn't it?" she asked.

"Yeah. Where is he now?"

"He's asleep, in my bed. I didn't want to disturb him. This has been a big day for him, getting—"

"I know," Jeremy said. "You already explained."

They were quiet for a moment, listening to the voices downstairs.

"Do you think they'll get a divorce?" Robin asked.

"No." But Jeremy knew how she felt. He used to worry about that, too. "Listen."

They both listened. Finally the voices stopped, and there was just silence downstairs.

"What's going on?" Robin asked.

"Shhh," Jeremy said. "Keep listening."

In a few moments they heard laughter, floating up the stairs.

14

*T*he doorbell woke up Jeremy on Saturday morning.

"Jeremy!" his mother called from downstairs. "One of your friends is here!"

Jeremy didn't know he had any friends who got up so early on Saturday mornings.

It was Andrew Blaney, the nose-picker.

"Hi, Germy," he said.

Jeremy rubbed his eyes.

"I wanted to get first pick," Andrew said.

Jeremy looked at him blankly. Was Andrew going to do something disgusting with his nose, right here in front of Jeremy's mother?

"Second pick, really," Andrew said. "I guess Squirrel already had first pick."

"Oh," Jeremy said. "The gerbils."

He took Andrew up to Robin's room. She had already dressed and made her bed. She was probably downstairs, fussing over George.

"Hey," Andrew said, bending over to see inside the gerbil cage, "these are neat."

Jeremy flopped onto Robin's bed. He pulled back the quilt and carefully slid down between the sheets. If he lay very still and didn't mess up the covers too much, Robin might not notice that he'd been there.

"Which one did Squirrel pick?" Andrew asked.

"What?" Jeremy said, still under the covers. "Oh, the biggest one."

"Then can I have this one?"

"I guess so," Jeremy said, without looking.

"Aren't you going to see which one I picked?" Andrew asked.

Jeremy got out of bed and looked. All of the babies looked the same. Only Bruno looked different because he was a little bigger than the others.

"Okay," Jeremy said again. "I see it."

"Aren't you going to mark it down?" Andrew asked.

Jeremy looked around for a sheet of paper, but Robin's room was immaculate and he couldn't find a thing. He went into his own room and found a math worksheet lying on the floor. He brought it back and wrote *Andrew Blaney*.

"There," he said.

Andrew looked at his name on the worksheet. "How will you know which gerbil is mine?" he asked.

Jeremy wrote *Second biggest—$2 deposit*. "How's that?" he asked.

"Fine," Andrew said. He took two crumpled bills out of his pocket and gave them to Jeremy.

This was his first deposit, but Jeremy tried to act casual about it. He stuck the bills inside the waistband of his pajamas and led Andrew downstairs.

"That was quick," Mrs. Bluett said when she saw them. She smiled at Andrew. "Don't you want to stay and have breakfast with Jeremy? It's nothing fancy, just cereal."

Andrew looked embarrassed. "Uh, no thanks," he said. "I've already eaten."

"Then why don't you just sit down here while Jeremy eats?" Mrs. Bluett asked. "It won't take long."

Andrew looked to Jeremy for help. It was awful when grown-ups assumed kids were friends just because they were the same age.

"We're not playing," Jeremy said. "Andrew was just picking out a gerbil."

"Oh," Mrs. Bluett said, catching on. "Did you find one you like, Andrew?"

Andrew nodded. "I made a deposit."

"You what?" Mrs. Bluett looked at Andrew, then Jeremy.

"I made a deposit," Andrew said again. "On the second biggest one."

Mrs. Bluett shook her head. "No, you didn't."

"I didn't?"

"Give him back the money, Jeremy," Mrs. Bluett said. "His mother has to call me first, remember?"

"But, Mom . . ."

"Give it back, Jeremy."

Jeremy took the bills out of his waistband.

"I want to make sure your mother knows what she's getting into," Mrs. Bluett explained.

"Oh, she knows," Andrew said. "I've had a gerbil before. His name was Theo."

"Really?" Mrs. Bluett said. "What happened to him?"

"He died," he said matter-of-factly. "My mother's boy-friend stepped on him, and he went splat."

Jeremy's mother shuddered. "How awful," she said.

"Yeah," Andrew said. "That's why I want to get this one. I'm going to name him Splat."

Mrs. Bluett looked at Andrew with distaste. "*If* you get a gerbil, you should pick a healthier name," she said, "and you should keep the poor thing in a cage so he won't get hurt."

"Oh, Theo was in a cage," Andrew said, "but he chewed his way out."

"Jeremy," Mrs. Bluett said, "go give the gerbils some more valentines."

But the doorbell rang just then. It was David Jones, wanting to pick a gerbil.

Altogether, thirteen kids came to pick out gerbils. Carl Castaldi was the last.

"I'll just have to put your name on the waiting list," Jeremy told him. "There are twelve kids ahead of you, thirteen counting Squirrel. So you'll have to wait for a couple of litters."

"Gee," Carl said. "I wish Big Mama would have her babies faster."

Jeremy did, too.

Andrew Blaney's mother called while the Bluetts were eating dinner.

"Well," Mrs. Bluett said on the telephone, "do you think he can keep it in the cage this time? . . . Oh, I see . . . Well, that's good."

When she got off the phone, Mrs. Bluett said Andrew's mother was planning to buy a wire cage this time. They'd had a plastic cage before, and Theo had chewed a hole in it.

"He had one of those beautiful plastic cages?" Robin said. "With tunnels and staircases and little balconies?"

"And holes," Mrs. Bluett said. "They're not so beautiful with holes in them."

"Oh." Robin looked disappointed, but relieved, too. She probably felt guilty about spending her money on George, instead of the gerbils.

"I feel better about letting Andrew have a gerbil," Mrs. Bluett said, "but I feel funny about making him pay for it."

"Maybe we should pay his mother for taking a gerbil off our hands," her husband suggested.

"Are you kidding?" Jeremy said. "These gerbils are valuable. Kids are lining up to buy them." He looked nervously at Robin. When was she going to claim some of the money?

But Robin surprised him.

"The gerbils aren't a business," she said righteously. "They're our pets."

Jeremy smiled. "They may be pets to you," he said, "but they're strictly business to me."

15

*I*t snowed the next day. Not very much, but enough for Robin to shovel two neighbors' sidewalks after it stopped. She probably would have shoveled more, but Mrs. Bluett made her come inside because she thought Robin was getting too cold.

When Robin came in, she laid two five-dollar bills on the table in front of Jeremy.

"*This* is a business," she said. "Not selling babies."

Jeremy tried not to look at the money. "Some people use their muscles to make money," he said, "and some people use their brains."

"How much money have you made with your brainy business?" Robin asked.

"It always takes a while for a new business to get started," he said.

Robin smiled.

Squirrel called that night.

"I've got bad news, Germy," he said.

"What?" Jeremy asked, with a sinking feeling. Squirrel didn't often have bad news, but when he did, it was usually awful.

"My mom won't let me have Bruno."

Jeremy's feelings stopped sinking. This might be bad news for Squirrel, but not for him. If Squirrel couldn't have Bruno, that meant somebody else could. Somebody who would pay five dollars.

Still, Jeremy tried to sound sympathetic. "Gee," he said, "didn't you tell her he's free?"

Squirrel sighed. "She said, 'You get what you pay for.' "

Andrew Blaney gave Jeremy his two-dollar reservation deposit on Monday morning. Jeremy folded the dollar bills carefully and put them in his pocket. He might as well keep the money himself until he had the full $10.55 to pay the school. Besides, the bills felt good in his pocket.

He asked other kids when they were going to pay their deposits.

"Soon," David Jones said. "Very soon."

"Probably tomorrow," Scott Richmond said.

"Don't forget that one of your parents has to call my mom first," Jeremy reminded them.

"Right." David nodded.

"No problem," said Scott.

Then Michael Taylor walked up with two new packs of baseball cards.

Jeremy had lots of baseball cards—1,842, not counting his Willie Mays rookie card—but they were all from last season, or from seasons before that. Michael's cards were for the new baseball season and showed the players' updated statistics.

"Hook's Drug Store just got them," Michael said. "I was in the store last night when they were putting them on the shelves."

"How much do they cost this year?" Jeremy asked. It was nice to be able to ask a question like that when he had money in his pocket.

"Forty-nine cents a pack," Michael said.

If Jeremy bought one pack—just one—he would still have $1.51 left to pay the school.

But Michael had two packs. And everyone else would buy two packs. Jeremy should buy at least two, maybe three.

❦

The reporter looks at Jeremy in dismay. "But, sir," he says, "I thought you always paid your debts!"

"I do," Jeremy says. "Eventually."

"Oh, sir . . ." The reporter's voice trails off, disappointed.

❦

The two dollar bills formed an uncomfortable lump in Jeremy's hip pocket. It was hard to sit still. He kept getting up to sharpen his pencil. When his pencil broke for the fourth time, he headed for the sharpener.

"Not again, Jeremy," Mrs. Scheeler said. "Stay in your seat."

Jeremy tried. But the lump in his pocket kept getting bigger and bigger.

Finally Jeremy raised his hand again.

"I told you, no more sharpening," Mrs. Scheeler said.

"It's not that," Jeremy said. "I have to go to the principal's office."

"What?" Mrs. Scheeler asked. Fifth graders didn't often ask to go to the principal's office.

"I have to go to the office," Jeremy said again.

"Are you sick?" she asked.

"No, I have to see Ms. Morrison."

A falsetto voice rose from the back of the room. "Kissy-face! Kissy-face!"

"That's enough, Kevin," Mrs. Scheeler said. Still puzzled, she turned back to Jeremy. "All right, but hurry back."

Jeremy didn't waste any time looking in classrooms or testing drinking fountains. He hurried to the office before he changed his mind.

"I need to see Ms. Morrison," he told the school secretary. "Right away."

Before the secretary had a chance to answer, Ms. Morrison called, "Come on in, Jeremy!" She evidently had extremely sharp hearing.

Jeremy went into the principal's office and plopped the two dollar bills on her desk.

"What's this?" Ms. Morrison asked.

"It's my first installment," he said. "I still owe eight dollars and fifty-five cents."

"Oh, Jeremy," she said, smiling. "You're *so* conscientious!"

She stood up and looked like she might hug him again, so Jeremy backed away.

Ms. Morrison held out the money. "But you don't have to pay me in bits and pieces," she said. "You can wait until you have all of the money."

"No," Jeremy said. "I can't."

Tears well up in the reporter's eyes. "You are an inspiration to honest businessmen everywhere, Mr. Bluett," he says.

16

*J*eremy didn't get any more reservation deposits.

"I'll pay the full amount when my gerbil is big enough to take home," Scott Richmond said.

Other kids nodded.

So Jeremy started checking the baby gerbils for signs of growth. They didn't look at all like pencil erasers anymore. But their eyes were still closed, and a layer of dark fuzz was just starting to show on their backs.

He could see that this growing business was going to take some time. Too much time.

He wanted money, lots of money, and he wanted it now.

"How old were you when you made your first million dollars, Mr. Bluett?" the reporter asks.

"Hmmm." Jeremy thinks for a moment. "I believe I was eleven."

"Eleven!" The reporter whistles. "That's awfully young!"

Jeremy smiles. "I was ready."

❧

Jeremy went to the hardware store on Saturday morning with his father. Next to the cash register was another can, with another picture of the kid with crutches, smiling bravely.

Mr. Bluett dropped some coins into the can, and they clunked satisfactorily against other coins. The can sounded almost full. With full cans all over town, that kid on crutches must be getting rich.

Maybe Jeremy could put his own picture on a can next to a cash register somewhere. With a bandage wrapped around his head and a crutch stuck under his armpit, he could look pretty tragic.

People would love it. They'd fill the can with coins—no, dollar bills—until Jeremy was the richest kid in the country. He practiced smiling bravely.

Then he looked back at the little girl on the can. Those crutches were real, and so was her smile.

Jeremy knew he couldn't do it. He would just have to wait for the gerbils to grow.

❧

Jeremy let Robin keep the gerbil cage in her room an extra week and then another week after that. One day, though, Robin insisted on bringing the cage back. Jeremy took one whiff, and he knew why Robin didn't want it in her room anymore.

"You told Mom you were going to clean the cage," Jeremy said.

"I've been busy," Robin said, "taking care of Georgie."

Jeremy had to sleep with his head under the pillow that night because the cage filled his room with a sour odor.

"Whew!" Mrs. Bluett said when she poked her head inside his room Friday morning. "It's time to clean that cage!"

"But we don't want to disturb the babies," Jeremy said.

"Disturb them?" Mrs. Bluett said. "If you don't disturb them, they won't be able to breathe!"

"Robin said she'd clean it," Jeremy said.

"And you said you'd help," Mrs. Bluett reminded him.

After they got home from Mrs. Carlson's that afternoon, Mrs. Bluett gave Jeremy and Robin a large cardboard box. "Put the gerbils in here while you clean the cage," she said.

The smell was even more powerful when they opened the lid. Jeremy stepped back for air while Robin lifted the gerbils out of the cage and placed them gently in the cardboard box. The babies' eyes were open now, and they had fur all over their bodies. Robin held them at a distance, because of the smell, but she still crooned over each one.

"Well, hello, Itsy," she said. "How are you today? And how is your brother Bitsy?"

"Itsy?" Jeremy said. "Bitsy?"

"Those are their names," Robin explained. "Here, do you want to hold one?"

"No," Jeremy said, barely breathing because of the smell. "I want to get this job done."

Robin smiled. "You're still scared of them, aren't you?"

"Me?" Jeremy started to laugh, but that would have meant inhaling too much of the foul air.

He picked up the empty cage and held it as far away from his nose as possible. Then, taking shallow breaths, he carried the cage outside and emptied the smelly cedar chips and valentine scraps into the trash can.

The cage still smelled sour, so he took it down to the

basement and rinsed it off in the sink next to the washing machine. He even poured Wisk over it. Then he dumped cedar chips into the bottom of the cage.

Jeremy sniffed the cage. It wasn't too bad, so he carried it back up to his room.

He found Robin had the babies out on the floor.

"What are you doing?" he cried.

"Letting them get some exercise," Robin said.

"Well, put them back in the cage," he ordered. "Now!"

"Don't worry," Robin said. "These are just babies, and they can't run very fast yet."

But when she put the babies back in the cage, there were only four.

"Uh oh," she said. "Itsy, Bitsy, Teeny, Tiny . . . where's Big Boy?"

Jeremy knew right away that Big Boy must be Bruno. And he was on the loose.

⤳

They looked under the bed, in the closet, and behind the furniture.

"I can't believe you let another one get away," Jeremy said.

"Don't worry," Robin said. "I always find them."

"*Always?*"

"They kept getting loose when they were in my room," she said. "Once I found Charlie in the bathroom, behind the toilet."

Jeremy used that toilet every day.

"If you were going to let Charlie out of the cage, at least you could have kept your door shut," Jeremy said.

"Oh, I did," Robin said. "But he can scoot right under the door, even when it's shut."

Jeremy went to the bathroom to look behind the toilet. But Bruno wasn't there.

"Maybe George can find him," Robin said. "The police on TV use dogs to find missing people all the time."

They found George asleep in the kitchen, and Robin carried him upstairs. She held him up to the gerbil cage.

"Get a good sniff," she said.

George sniffed.

"Okay, Georgie," she said, setting him on the floor. "Find Big Boy!"

George sat down.

"Go, Georgie!" she said. "Find Big Boy!"

George just sat.

"This isn't working," Jeremy said. "I think the police use more energetic dogs."

George lay down and put his head on his paws.

"George has plenty of energy," Robin said. "The problem is, you washed away Big Boy's smell. Now the cage just smells like laundry detergent."

"Then why doesn't he lead us to the washing machine?" Jeremy asked.

"He's not stupid," Robin said. "He knows gerbils can't go down stairs."

They looked for the missing baby all afternoon. They tried to be casual about the search because they didn't want their mother to know a rodent was loose in her house.

Still, Mrs. Bluett knew something was wrong.

"What's going on?" she asked at dinner. "You two have been looking over your shoulders all afternoon. It's almost as if someone were chasing you."

"They've got the fidgets," Mr. Bluett said. "Don't you remember getting the fidgets when you were a kid?"

"Not like that," his wife said.

Jeremy and Robin kept looking for Bruno all evening. While their parents watched television, they looked in the linen closet, the clothes hamper, even in their parents' shower stall.

"He's not here," Robin said. "I bet he's back in that messy closet of yours."

"We'd hear him if he were there," Jeremy said. "Remember how Charlie rattled the Cheetos bag?"

"Maybe he's trapped. Maybe he can't move." Robin looked like she was going to cry.

But Jeremy thought a trapped gerbil was better than one that could sneak up on him and chew off his toes.

"Do you think we should tell Mom?" Robin asked.

Jeremy thought about it. "I don't think she'd want to know," he said truthfully.

"But what will he eat?" Robin worried. "He'll starve without Big Mama's milk!"

Jeremy wondered if a starving gerbil could get vicious.

"Maybe we should set out a bowl of milk for him," he said. He had no idea whether a gerbil would drink milk from a bowl, but Robin seemed to think so. She went downstairs to get some milk.

Jeremy looked around his room one more time. Then he tucked the blankets tightly around his mattress, just in case Bruno tried to slip in between the sheets during the night.

17

*I*n the morning the milk looked untouched.

"Oh no!" Robin cried. "He hasn't eaten!" She looked at Jeremy's closet. "He's trapped in there," she said. "I just know it."

Jeremy looked at his closet, too. "You're probably right," he admitted.

"Do you think he's already dead?" Robin asked softly.

"I hope not." Jeremy certainly didn't want a dead gerbil in his closet. That was almost as bad as a live one. But there was only one way to be sure. "I'll clean my closet," he said.

"You would do that for Big Boy?" Robin said, impressed.

"His name is Bruno."

"Right," Robin said, still grateful. "Bruno."

Jeremy began after breakfast. He filled three trash bags

with old test papers, empty Cheetos bags, baseball card wrappers, and unusual objects that he had once thought valuable. He worked carefully and quickly, just in case Bruno was lying in wait for him. He looked inside his shoes, shook out his old pumpkin costume, and even checked inside his violin case.

Robin hauled away the trash bags.

"What's with the trash bags?" Mrs. Bluett asked from the hall.

"Jeremy's cleaning his closet," Robin said.

"Really?" Mrs. Bluett looked in Jeremy's room and beamed at the sight. Then the glow left her face and was replaced by a more familiar look. "Why are you doing this?" she asked suspiciously.

"My closet was messy," Jeremy said.

Amazingly, his mother believed that.

"I guess you're growing up," she said, smiling again. "Now let's see if you can keep it like this."

"I will," Jeremy promised. He intended to keep his whole room neat, at least until Bruno showed up. He also intended to keep his shoes on.

Mr. Bluett came up the stairs with a newspaper in his hand. "Who did this?" he asked, holding up the front page of *The Columbus Dispatch*. Only the masthead didn't say *The Columbus Dispatch*. It said *The Colu   spatch*.

Jeremy had seen enough shredded valentines to recognize the work of a gerbil.

"Where'd you find it?" he asked.

"In the family room, just where I left it," his father said.

Robin and Jeremy looked at each other. Obviously gerbils *could* go down stairs.

"I don't mind you looking at these papers, but I wish you'd be careful with them," Mr. Bluett said. "I have to take them back to the office for other people to read."

"Oh, Hank," his wife said, "don't be such a fussbudget. It probably got ripped in the mail."

"No, it didn't," Mr. Bluett said. "I remember."

"Oh, Hank . . ."

They carried their argument downstairs, and Robin turned to Jeremy with a grin. "He can chew!" she said. "Big Boy— I mean, Bruno—won't starve!"

Jeremy and Robin waited until their parents were in the kitchen before they began searching the family room. They started in the stack of out-of-town newspapers that their father kept by his chair. *The Cleveland Plain Dealer* and *The Indianapolis Star* had big holes in them, too.

"Bruno must be very hungry," Robin said.

They looked behind the TV, under the couch, and behind every book on the shelf.

Jeremy was checking under a sofa cushion and Robin had the XYZ volume of the encyclopedia in her hand when their mother appeared at the door of the family room.

"What on earth are you two doing?" she asked.

Robin looked at Jeremy.

"I'm helping Robin with a school project," he said.

"Really?" Mrs. Bluett beamed again. "What's your project, Robin?"

"Uh . . ."

Jeremy looked at the XYZ encyclopedia in her hand. "It's on zebras," he said. "Zoos and zebras."

His mother cocked her head and looked at him. "You seem to know more about her project than she does," she said.

Jeremy smiled. "I told you, I'm helping her."

Mrs. Bluett smiled back. "First cleaning your closet, and now helping your sister. This almost makes up for the mess you left in the kitchen."

"What mess?"

"The spilled cereal," she said. "But don't worry. If you can clean your closet *and* help your sister, I guess I can take care of a little mess on the kitchen table."

Jeremy still didn't remember spilling any cereal. But Mrs. Bluett went back to the kitchen, and he decided not to worry about it.

Until he heard his mother scream.

18

Jeremy and Robin ran to the kitchen. George waddled in behind them.

"A rat!" Mrs. Bluett cried, pointing to the box of Rice Krispies on the kitchen table. "A rat!"

Mr. Bluett picked up the cereal box. "There's nothing in here, Sal."

"Of course not," she said evenly. "He jumped out when I picked up the box. But it was a rat, I tell you, a *rat*."

Mr. Bluett looked at the box. Then he looked at Jeremy and Robin.

"About the size of a gerbil?" he asked.

"Oh no," Mrs. Bluett said. "It was much bigger than that. It was a *rat*."

"A rat couldn't fit inside this box," Mr. Bluett said reasonably.

"Okay, it was a *little* rat," Mrs. Bluett said. "But it was in this box." Then she looked at Robin and Jeremy, too. "Maybe it *was* a gerbil. A big fat gerbil."

"No," Robin said. "It was just a little baby gerbil."

Mrs. Bluett stared at her. "A little baby gerbil? A gerbil is loose in this house, and you didn't tell me?"

"Jeremy didn't think you'd want to know."

Jeremy smiled at his mother, the same way he had when she'd found him cleaning his closet and helping Robin with her report. But this time she didn't smile back.

"Where'd he go, Sal?" Mr. Bluett asked. "That's what we need to know now."

"I don't know," she said. "Somewhere over there." She waved in the direction of the kitchen sink, and they all noticed that the cabinet door beneath the sink was slightly ajar. Mr. Bluett snapped the cabinet door shut.

"All right," he said, rubbing his hands together. "We know where he is, and he can't get away. If we all work together, we'll catch this little guy in no time, no time at all."

"I am *not* touching a rodent," his wife said.

"You won't have to," Mr. Bluett said. "We'll just create barriers, and trap him. Jeremy, give me the Rice Krispies."

Jeremy handed his father the cereal box, and Mr. Bluett placed it on its side in front of the cabinet door.

"That's good," Mr. Bluett said, "but I need more. A lot more."

Jeremy started opening cabinets and handing boxes to his father. Some of the boxes were boring, like the boxes of Shredded Wheat and nonfat dry milk. But some were very interesting, like the boxes of cheese crackers and chocolate fudge brownie mix.

Mr. Bluett stacked the boxes in a tower around the cabinet where the gerbil was. Then he opened the cabinet door.

Nothing happened.

"Maybe he's not in there," Robin said.

"He's in there, all right," Mr. Bluett said. "We just have to wait."

They all stood around the cabinet door, waiting.

Still, nothing happened.

"Maybe I'll have to go in there and flush him out," Mr. Bluett said. "Give me the broom."

Jeremy gave him the broom, and Mr. Bluett poked the handle around inside the cabinet.

Still, nothing happened.

They all heard a soft, scratching noise.

"Look," Robin said, pointing to the windowsill above the sink.

There was Bruno, sitting on his hind legs and watching them.

"Oh," Mrs. Bluett said weakly. "I'll never enjoy looking out that window again."

"But he's so cute!" Robin started to reach for Bruno, but Mr. Bluett pulled her arm back.

"We've got to build a barrier," he said, picking up the box of nonfat dry milk.

"No, we don't," she said, reaching for Bruno again. She put her hand on the sill, about six inches away from the gerbil.

"Don't do that!" her father said. "You'll scare him away!"

Bruno looked at her hand, interested.

"Give me a Rice Krispie," she said softly.

Jeremy gave her a Rice Krispie.

She put it on the palm of her hand and held it very still. Bruno looked at it a moment, then stepped onto her hand.

Gently, Robin withdrew her hand from the windowsill. "Bruno, Bruno, Bruno," she crooned. "You had us all *very* worried. I thought you might have fallen down the garbage disposal."

Mrs. Bluett turned pale and put her hand over her mouth. "I never even thought of that. What if I had turned it on?"

While Robin stroked Bruno with her fingertip, the gerbil held the Rice Krispie between his front paws and chewed on it.

Mrs. Bluett took her hand away from her mouth. "Throw away the Rice Krispies," she said. "I never want to have Rice Krispies in the house again."

"Calm down, Sal," Mr. Bluett said. "All's well that ends well."

Mrs. Bluett shook her head. "All's well that ends in a pet shop."

"But, Mom . . ." Robin began.

"No buts about it," Mrs. Bluett said. "That gerbil can *chew*. He and his brothers and sisters have to go to the pet store." She looked at Jeremy. "Today."

"What about all the kids that want them?" Jeremy asked.

"Get serious, Jeremy," she said. "Nobody wants these things. Or if they do, their parents don't."

"What about Andrew Blaney? He's already paid a deposit."

"Give it back."

"I can't. I already gave the money to Ms. Morrison." He paused. "To pay off my debt."

"You did?" She looked surprised. "You didn't buy any Big Bubba or baseball cards or football helmets or . . ."

Jeremy kept shaking his head.

"Well," she said. "Well."

"Can't we wait, just until Monday, to take the gerbils back?"

"Well," said his mother, obviously impressed by the fact that he'd used Andrew's deposit to pay his school debt. "I guess we can wait until Monday. But no longer. If kids want gerbils, their parents will have to call me at work Monday afternoon. As soon as I get home, these things are going to the pet store."

She put on rubber gloves and filled the kitchen sink with suds. Then she began scrubbing the windowsill.

19

*J*eremy called Andrew Blaney, who came over to pick up his gerbil Sunday afternoon. Andrew brought his money in an envelope.

While Jeremy checked to make sure three dollars were in the envelope, Robin said good-bye to the gerbil. "Oh, Itsy!" she cried. "I'll really miss you!"

"Itsy?" Andrew asked.

"That's his name," Robin said.

"Maybe that *was* his name," Andrew said. "Now his name is Splat."

"Splat?" Robin asked.

"Yeah, see, I used to have a gerbil and he . . ."

But Jeremy didn't think Robin should hear that story. "I thought you said you were going to give him a healthier name," he told Andrew.

"Your mother's the one who said that," Andrew said. "Don't worry, though. Splat'll be fine."

"Don't forget to give him a sunflower seed every morning," Robin said. "He really likes sunflower seeds."

"Right," Andrew said.

❧

Jeremy couldn't find his left shoe on Monday morning. Mr. Bluett had already left for work, but Mrs. Bluett and Robin helped him look for it. Jeremy couldn't find his sneakers, either, and Mrs. Bluett talked about sending him to school barefoot.

But Robin finally found the shoe in one of the trash bags she had hauled from Jeremy's closet on Saturday morning.

"See?" Jeremy said. "That just shows how dangerous it is to clean a closet."

"We'll talk about this later," his mother said grimly.

Because he was late, Jeremy didn't have time to ask anyone about the gerbils in the morning. But he confronted David Jones and Scott Richmond in the cafeteria line at noon.

"Why haven't your parents called about the gerbils?" he asked.

"Well . . ." David's eyes traveled around the cafeteria.

"Well?" Jeremy demanded.

David looked Jeremy straight in the eye. "Actually, she decided about two weeks ago."

"And?" But Jeremy already knew what the decision was.

"She says she doesn't like rodents," David said. "She says she'll move out if a rodent moves in."

"That's exactly what my dad said," Scott said. "He says rodents give him the creeps."

Jeremy asked three other boys, who said their parents

wouldn't let them buy gerbils, either. Jeremy took his tray to a space that Squirrel had saved for him.

"Why doesn't anyone want my gerbils?" he moaned.

"We want them," Squirrel said, "but our parents don't."

"What's wrong with these parents?" Jeremy asked.

Before Squirrel could answer, Kevin Johansen came up and set his tray next to Jeremy's. "Mind if I sit down, guys?"

They didn't say anything, and he sat down.

"So, Germy, my boy," Kevin said. "I hear you're having trouble dumping the gerbils."

"They're not ready to leave their mother yet," Jeremy lied. "Their eyes aren't even open yet."

Kevin laughed. "Do you think they'll be more popular when their eyes are open?"

"I'm not worried," Jeremy lied again, then found something true to say: "Andrew Blaney already bought one."

"That nose-picker?" Kevin laughed again. "You'll have to pay anyone else to take them."

"No, I won't," Jeremy said. "I've already had to turn down an offer."

"Yeah? Whose offer?" Kevin jutted out his chin.

Jeremy jutted his, too. "Buckeye Pets," he said. "The manager practically begged."

Kevin brought his chin back in. "Sure, Germy," he said. "Sure."

"Does Kevin do a good job of cleaning the toilets in your mansion?" the reporter asks.

Jeremy hesitates. "Well, I must admit that sometimes I have to make him go back and clean one again. In fact, I remember one time when he had to clean the same toilet bowl seventeen times before it passed inspection."

104

"You must have very high standards," the reporter says admiringly.

"Did Buckeye Pets really offer to buy the gerbils?" Squirrel asked on the way home from school.

"Not *buy*," Jeremy said. "The guy said he'd take them, but he wouldn't give me any money for them."

"That's better than nothing," Squirrel said.

"Not much," Jeremy said. "Remember, I still owe the school five dollars and fifty-five cents." He had given Ms. Morrison the three dollars Andrew had paid for his gerbil.

"Somebody's parents will call," Squirrel assured him.

"They'd better call fast," Jeremy said. "My mom says we have to take the babies to the pet store this afternoon."

"Maybe your mom will change her mind," Squirrel said. "Maybe she'll feel sorry for you and give you another chance to sell the gerbils."

"I don't think so," Jeremy said, remembering that his mother had been willing to send him to school barefoot that morning.

"Then maybe she'll feel sorry for Robin," Squirrel said. "Robin really likes those gerbils."

But Mrs. Bluett showed no pity, not even for Robin.

"I don't want to find a gerbil in a box of cereal again," she said.

"But these are our *babies*," Robin said tearfully.

"The pet store will find good homes for them," her mother said. "And, besides, Big Mama will give us more babies soon enough."

Robin wiped her tears. "Promise?"

Her mother sighed. "I'm afraid so."

The man at Buckeye Pets gave them a free bag of rodent food in exchange for the baby gerbils.

"We'd rather have cash," Jeremy said.

"No, we wouldn't," Mrs. Bluett said quickly. "We still have to feed Big Mama and Charlie, not to mention George. We're just thankful that we don't have to pay you to take them."

The man laughed. "I'm always glad to get gerbils."

"Make sure you find good homes for them," Robin said.

The man nodded and laughed again. He evidently didn't know how hard it would be to sell these gerbils.

20

Squirrel ran to meet Jeremy in the school parking lot the next morning. "Germy! Germy! You won't believe it!"

"What?"

"My mom changed her mind! She says I can have Bruno after all!"

"But we already gave him to the pet store."

"Well, can't you get him back?"

"I don't know."

"Call and ask!"

"Okay, but what made her change her mind?" Jeremy asked.

"I told her how much I wanted Bruno."

"I thought you told her that before."

"This time she believed me."

Jeremy knew Squirrel's tricks with his mother. "You cried, didn't you?"

Squirrel just grinned.

⌒⌒

Jeremy called Buckeye Pets from the phone in his parents' bedroom. The same man answered.

"My name is Jeremy Bluett," Jeremy said. "And I brought four baby gerbils into your store yesterday."

"Sure, I remember," the man said. "I gave you some free rodent food."

"Yeah, well, I was wondering if I could have one of the gerbils back," Jeremy said.

The man didn't say anything.

"See, a friend of mine wants it."

"Then tell him to come in and buy one."

"No, see, he wants one gerbil in particular. One that we gave you yesterday. He's already named it and everything."

"Well, I don't have the gerbils you gave me anymore."

"You don't?"

"No, but I bet your friend won't know the difference if you give him another one. All gerbils look pretty much the same."

Jeremy couldn't believe Buckeye Pets had sold all four gerbils already, in less than a day.

"How'd you do it?" he asked.

"What?" asked the man.

"How'd you sell the gerbils so fast? I couldn't get anybody to buy them."

"Oh," the man said. "I didn't sell them. I fed them to the snakes."

"You what?"

"We've got a large snake collection."

Jeremy felt something slither through his stomach.

"When I get new gerbils, I like to give them to the snakes right away," the man said.

Bruno had been eaten by a snake.

But the man just kept on talking. "That way I don't have to mix them with the gerbils I already have. Sometimes they get into fights when you mix them."

Bitsy and Teeny and Tiny, too. Eaten by snakes.

At least Itsy was safe, sort of, with Andrew Blaney.

"Kid?" The man's voice came over the telephone wire. "Are you still there?"

Jeremy found his voice. "Yes," he said weakly.

"Well, I gotta go," the man said. "I've got a customer waiting."

The phone clicked, but Jeremy still sat there, holding the receiver to his ear.

Maybe the man was kidding. Maybe he just didn't want to give back Bruno.

But maybe he wasn't kidding.

Jeremy hung up the phone and went downstairs to the kitchen, where his parents were fixing dinner and Robin was opening a can of dog food.

"Dad," he said.

"Yo," said his father, chopping lettuce.

"What do snakes eat?" Jeremy asked.

Mrs. Bluett stirred a lemon-pimiento chicken sauce on the stove. "What a question," she said. "And right before dinner."

But Robin looked interested. "Why? Are you thinking about getting a snake?"

"No," Mrs. Bluett said. "He's not even thinking about it. He wouldn't dare."

Jeremy shrugged. "I just wanted to know what snakes eat."

"Oh, lots of things," his father said. "Bugs and mice and stuff like that."

"Do you think they'd eat a gerbil?"

Mr. Bluett stopped chopping, and Mrs. Bluett stopped stirring.

"Why?" Mr. Bluett asked. "What happened?"

"Well . . ."

Mrs. Bluett couldn't wait. "Just tell me this: Is there a snake in this house?"

"No."

She sat down, relieved.

"Then what?" Mr. Bluett asked.

Jeremy looked at Robin. "I don't think I should tell you here."

"Did a snake eat one of my babies?" Robin asked.

"Well . . ."

Robin began to cry.

&

Robin stayed up in her room during dinner. Jeremy didn't feel much like eating, either.

"What's this thing?" Jeremy asked, poking at a small red object that looked like a little pink eraser, only darker.

"A pimiento," his mother said. "It won't kill you."

But she picked at her food, too.

"I think the pet store manager should have told us what he was planning to do with the gerbils," she said. "That would have been the decent thing to do."

"Would that have changed anything?" Mr. Bluett asked. "I mean, we still had to get rid of them."

Jeremy and his mother stared at Mr. Bluett. But they knew he was right.

"I just hate to think that we're raising little animals for slaughter," Mrs. Bluett said. "Even if they are disgusting little animals."

"Well, if it's any comfort, I can assure you that the babies weren't slaughtered," Mr. Bluett said. "I've seen snakes eat, and they're very neat about it. They swallow their prey alive, so there's very little blood. The snake—"

"Hank, please."

"—doesn't even chew," he said. "He just opens his mouth wide and—"

"*Hank!*"

"Oh, right." Mr. Bluett looked around. "I guess we shouldn't talk about stuff like this while we're eating."

Jeremy just looked at the pimiento on his plate.

After dinner Jeremy went up to his room and lay on his bed, thinking of Bruno. He'd been the biggest pink eraser in the litter. The one who'd followed Big Mama when she got tired of nursing. The one who'd sat on the windowsill, watching.

He thought of Bitsy and Teeny and Tiny, too. But mostly he thought of Bruno.

Swallowed alive.

"Don't feel too bad, sir," the reporter says. "He had a good life."

"What makes you think that?" Jeremy asks.

"He knew you loved him."

Jeremy shakes his head. "I didn't love him. I just wanted to sell him. For money."

"But you must have liked him a little bit," the reporter insists.

Jeremy shakes his head again. "I never even touched him."

"Oh," the reporter says. "That's sad."

Later he heard Robin go downstairs. He got up and went into her room. He knelt by the gerbils' cage. Somehow, he felt he should tell Big Mama what had happened.

He should apologize.

Then he noticed that Big Mama was shredding valentines with her teeth.

She was building a new nest.

21

"*R*obin!" Jeremy called downstairs. "Come quick!"

Robin didn't answer.

"Robin!" he called again. "Big Mama's building another nest!"

"What?" Robin came to the foot of the stairs.

"Big Mama's building another nest," he repeated.

"More babies!" she squealed, running up the stairs. Then she stopped. "Oh no. What'll we do?"

"I don't know," Jeremy said.

But he knew they couldn't let Big Mama go on, having litter after litter after litter. Not when her babies were going to be eaten by snakes.

"We'd better make sure this is her last litter," he said.

"We'd better buy a new cage, to keep Charlie and Big Mama apart, so they won't have any more babies."

"But we can't buy a cage," Robin said. "I don't have any money."

"What happened to the ten dollars you made shoveling snow?" Jeremy asked.

"I spent it," Robin said. "Georgie needed a brush and some shampoo and . . ."

Oh well, ten dollars wouldn't have been enough anyway.

Robin looked out the window. "Maybe it'll snow again. Maybe I can make some more money."

But Jeremy knew they needed more than a maybe. They needed a sure thing, and they needed it now, before the new babies appeared and Charlie started chasing Big Mama again.

There was only one sure thing.

"I'll sell my Willie Mays rookie card," he said.

Robin started to laugh. "You? Sell Willie Mays?"

"I'll buy another Willie Mays rookie card someday," Jeremy told her. "One without Coke stains."
gerbils?"

Jeremy thought of Bruno, and nodded.

"Oh, Germy," Robin said softly. She looked at him the way she used to, back when she was just a little kid and thought Jeremy was the most wonderful person in the world.

"I'll buy another Willy Mays rookie card someday," Jeremy told her. "One without Coke stains."

"Maybe I can buy it for you," Robin said.

Jeremy smiled at her. Robin was okay.

She patted her dresser top. "We can put the new cage right here," she said. "That way Big Mama and Charlie can live next door to each other." She looked at Jeremy. "Unless you want one of them in your room?"

"No," Jeremy said quickly. "They'd probably like to wave to each other every now and then."

"That's right," Robin said. "They can wave. But no more babies!"

Except for the ones that were already on the way. And Jeremy had to figure out what to do with those.

∞

Jeremy saw Squirrel on the playground the next morning. He decided to tell him outright.

"Bruno's dead."

"What?"

"A snake ate him."

Squirrel whistled softly. "Geez Louise. How'd that happen?"

"The pet store manager fed him to a snake. He fed all of the baby gerbils to snakes. They're all dead."

"Geez Louise," Squirrel said again.

"And that's not all," Jeremy said. "Big Mama's going to have another litter."

"Good," Squirrel said. "I'll take one of her new babies."

Jeremy looked at him. "But what about Bruno?"

"You just told me, a snake ate him."

Jeremy sighed. Squirrel was right. What was done, was done.

"But what about the new babies, the ones you don't take?" he asked. "What will happen to them?"

"I guess a snake'll eat them, too," Squirrel said.

"No," Jeremy said firmly. "I've got to find homes for them."

"Maybe you could advertise in *The Advocate-Journal*," Squirrel suggested. "That's how my mom sold our old dining room set."

"Ads cost too much," Jeremy said. "I checked when I was trying to sell my violin."

The first bell rang, and they began walking toward the school building.

"Can't your dad get the ad for free?" Squirrel asked.

Jeremy shook his head. "He says he just works for the newspaper. He doesn't own it."

"Too bad," Squirrel said.

Jeremy shrugged. "That's how the free enterprise system works."

Suddenly he stopped walking.

"That's it!" he cried.

"What?" Squirrel asked.

"If I owned a newspaper, I could run all the ads I wanted!"

"Yeah," Squirrel said. "And if I owned a spaceship, I could fly to the moon anytime I wanted."

"Don't you see?" Jeremy grabbed Squirrel's arm. "If I owned a newspaper, I'd be *part* of the free enterprise system! People would pay *me* to run ads!"

"But you don't own a newspaper," Squirrel pointed out.

"I could start one," Jeremy said. "I could start a school newspaper."

"A school newspaper?"

"Sure, I could report what's going on at school. And I could run ads!"

"I bet they won't let you run ads in a school newspaper," Squirrel said. "Remember, Mrs. Scheeler wouldn't let Kevin sell Twinkies on school property."

"A newspaper is different," Jeremy said. "Besides, I don't really need ads. I can write stories about the poor homeless gerbils that are going to be eaten by a snake." He thought of *The Advocate-Journal*'s story about the family whose house burned down. "People always like to help out when they read about a tragedy."

Squirrel still looked skeptical. "Doesn't it cost money to print a newspaper?" he asked.

"Yes, but I could charge everybody, say, a dollar a copy."

"A dollar?" Squirrel shook his head. "That's more than *The Advocate-Journal* costs."

"Okay," Jeremy said. "Fifty cents."

Squirrel kept shaking his head.

"Twenty-five?"

Squirrel still looked doubtful.

"Fifteen cents," Jeremy said firmly. "And that's my final offer."

"I wonder how much money you'll lose," Squirrel said.

"I won't lose a cent," Jeremy said. "This newspaper will make me *rich*."

He could see it now. A thick newspaper with news stories, comics, and maybe even some ads. He bet he could talk Ms. Morrison into letting him run a few ads.

He'd call the newspaper *The Dolley Madison Free Enterprise*.

No, some kids would think the paper was free. He'd better just call it *The Dolley Madison Enterprise*.

And he'd print 15 CENTS, in big letters, right under the title.

⤴

"Gee, Mr. Bluett," the reporter says. "Can I have a job?"

Rebecca C. Jones has written several highly acclaimed children's books, including an earlier book about Jeremy entitled *Germy Blew It!* and the novel *The Believers*. A former newspaper and television reporter, Ms. Jones currently divides her time between writing and teaching journalism. She lives in Annapolis, Maryland.

DON'T MAKE ME SMILE

by Barbara Park

The way Charlie Hickle sees it, there's no reason to smile. His parents are getting a divorce, and there doesn't seem to be anything he can do about it. Not that Charlie doesn't try. He does everything he can think of to convince his parents that he'll go nuts if they get a divorce. He threatens to spend the rest of his life in a tree. He refuses to eat his mother's cooking. He causes trouble in school and makes rude comments about his father's new apartment. With a little help from a new friend, though, Charlie finally starts to accept the inevitable changes in his life—but not until he makes a hilarious last-ditch effort to get his parents back together.

"Funny and touching—a good read."
—*Children's Book Review Service*

"The author does make you smile, proving that there is still room for one more middle-grade problem novel on divorce." —*Booklist*

BULLSEYE BOOKS PUBLISHED BY ALFRED A. KNOPF

MY MOTHER GOT MARRIED
(and Other Disasters)

by Barbara Park

Just when things were starting to get better for Charlie Hickle, they start to get worse all over again. First his mom decides to remarry, and then her new husband moves in...with his two kids! It's bad enough having teenaged Lydia hogging the bathroom and the phone, but her five-year-old brother, Thomas, is even more annoying. Thomas is a major-league pest who wants more than anything to be Charlie's friend. Worse, he's Charlie's new roommate. Charlie is convinced that his life is ruined. But after some time, and some very funny escapades, Charlie begins to learn that having siblings—even if they *are* step-siblings—is not as awful as it might seem.

"Refreshing...as hilarious as it is touching. A delight for all readers."   —*Publishers Weekly*

"A superb job. A story of surprising depth." —*Booklist*

BULLSEYE BOOKS PUBLISHED BY ALFRED A. KNOPF

ROBBIE AND THE LEAP YEAR BLUES

by Norma Klein

Robbie thinks his life is tough enough as it is. He's eleven and his parents are divorced, but they live in the same building. Half of the time Robbie can't even remember which apartment he's supposed to be living in. But then things get worse—Robbie develops girl trouble. Robbie thinks it's bad enough when Eve, a girl at school, asks him to marry her. But then a big mix-up lands Robbie at his mom's boyfriend's house for the weekend, and his daughter Tracie decides *she* likes Robbie too! Robbie wasn't sure he was ready for one girlfriend—and he sure doesn't know what to do now that he's got two!

"An accurate, humorous picture of 'modern' relationships."
                                        —*Publishers Weekly*

"Joint custody has never been so funny!"
                                        —*School Library Journal*

BULLSEYE BOOKS PUBLISHED BY ALFRED A. KNOPF